The Egg in the Crate

The Egg in the Crate

April Smith

The Egg in the Crate
Copyright © 2022 by April Smith

All rights reserved. No part of this publication may be reproduced, distributed, or transmitted in any form or by any means, including photocopying, recording, or other electronic or mechanical methods, without the prior written permission of the publisher or author, except in the case of brief quotations embodied in critical reviews and certain other noncommercial uses permitted by copyright law.

Although every precaution has been taken to verify the accuracy of the information contained herein, the author and publisher assume no responsibility for any errors or omissions. No liability is assumed for damages that may result from the use of information contained within.

Library of Congress Control Number: 2020904169
ISBN-13: Paperback: 978-1-64674-176-2
          PDF: 978-1-64398-312-7
          ePub: 978-1-64398-313-4
          Kindle: 978-1-64398-314-1

Printed in the United States of America

LitFire LLC
1-800-511-9787
www.litfirepublishing.com
order@litfirepublishing.com

This book is supposed to get you thinking of 4 different points: #1: How great our God is to teach the lost about Him. Example: David is a young man who tended sheep, but by the grace of God defeated a terrible giant. #2: Lazarus was sick in bed, he died while Mary went to get God and God waited and then came and brought him back from the dead. 3: God sometimes allows us to defeat monsters. Look at the example of David and Goliath again. Goliath was a giant, and everyone but God thought that he was going to die. David obeyed God and he defeated the monster. #3: God sometimes allows us to defeat monsters. Look at the example of David and Goliath again. Goliath was a giant, and everyone but God thought that he was going to die. David obeyed God and he defeated the monster. #4: Noah was a Christian who obeyed God. He built and ark and his friends were making fun of him. The floods came, he saves the animals and his family.

I hope that this book makes you think about all of these points, because it sure has me thinking about them all the time and how I pray. This book is one of my favorites, not just because I wrote it, but also because while I started writing, these points popped into my head, and I had to write them down. Once God put's something in my head, I keep thinking about it until He inspires me with the words to write down.

May God bless everyone, even if they don't enjoy my beautiful book. I might not be the best author, but I love writing. And with God, family, and friends on my side, there is no way I'm ever going to give up on this book or on any of my dreams; because, without God, I wouldn't have ever had the dream to be an author. I also am thankful for my high school teachers, because they presented a journalism class where I could write stories or even read a book and offer my viewpoints.

Once, there was an old castle that was built during the eighteenth century. The castle was very strong and had a king living in it, his name was King Chris. He was a cruel king that beat his slaves and anybody else who came there.

The knights and everybody else grew very angry. They wanted King Chris dead. The knights had heard about a crate with a monster's egg in it. A distinguished gentleman, known as the blue knight, ventured off to locate the crate.

After he found the crate, he made sure that the label read: "For the king". King Chris opened the crate and saw the egg. He grew mad and thought that the miners robbed him of his gold. He sent his knights to the mine and told them to cut off their heads. While the knights were on their mission, King Chris kept the egg in the crate and it hatched. The monster came out of the egg and crawled around.

The monster found a cat and ate it; then it grew about a foot. The monster named itself Creepy because it had previously crept around for about an hour before it had come to a hole full of rats and mice. Creepy ate all of the rats and mice, then vomited to rid itself of all the waste.

Creepy used her tall tentacles to help her stand up. Then she stood up and walked around until she came to the king. The king was asleep so he didn't notice Creepy coming to eat him, until it was too late. Creepy was now as tall as a full grown athlete. The knights that wanted King Chris dead congratulated the monster by letting her take over the castle.

After about ten years, they forgot about Creepy and did not feed her. She was starving so she ate small prey like rats, mice and spiders. The monster had become small again and not seen very often. The knights thought that she had died.

A few months later, a man and his family inquired as to the best place to move his family. The knights told him that the castle would be that place to move. The family moved in and started to clean and unpack. The family consisted of six girls, a father, and a mother. The girl's names were Rosecena, Tiger, Sam, Kim, Rose, and Vickie. At least that's what they told everyone. The mother's name was Belle, and the father's name was Troy Athlete. The father was a paleontologist, and the mother was a lawyer and a doctor. The girls loved to hang out together.

The whole family loved animals. They also went to church when they had the chance. They really enjoyed everything except when people fought or cursed each other out. After they moved in and started to work on cleaning the house, Rose and Sam went outside to the garden. They were very good at planting anything and everything.

The girls loved to go to parties, and they loved to watch movies. The only time the girls were apart was when they had to be, which is when Rosecena needed to hunt monsters or other creatures or even take a bath. They read books all the time except when they were too busy or too tired. They also loved to go shopping together for clothes, shoes, and video games.

Rosecena was the oldest and then came Vickie. Next, were Tiger and then Sam, Kim, and lastly Rose. Rosecena was an all-creatures slayer; Tiger did gymnastics, and Vickie was a teacher's assistant.

Rose was on the track team, and Sam wanted to be a vetenarian when she grows up enough. Kim was a baby, so no one knew what she was going to be. The sisters were all best friends. They played together every day. One day, some kids were picking on Rose; Tiger didn't know because she wasn't paying attention, but Rosecena noticed and went into action right away.

Rosecena saw Rose being picked on, and she told her sisters to come with her. They all went over to the girls that were picking on Rose. Rosecena was ready to fight when the principal came up and asked, "Is there a problem here?" They all said no and walked off and set off for their classes.

They were in different grades, but they always hung out together after class. On her first day of school, Rosecena was in gym class and was trying out to be a cheerleader. She was really good at it and became head cheerleader and the most popular girl in school. She also cared a lot about her family and tried to make their school life better for them.

When they arrived at their house, the sisters found a crate, and the crate had a note on it. It told them that they need to get the crate into the house and keep whatever is inside not to be broken. Rosecena then asked Kim if she could pick up the crate and get it into the house.

Kim picked up the crate and carried it inside very carefully so that she would not damage the crate or its contents. Just then, the phone rang. Rosecena ran and grabbed the phone. It was Harry, and he said "an accident has happened, and your father is trapped in a tomb with a mummy in it". Shortly afterwards, the tomb fell to the ground.

"The scientists are working on digging him out", he said, "but we fear the worst. "Call your mom and ask her to come to Egypt immediately." She was about to hang up when he said "Hey did a crate arrive there? Please check and make sure everything is okay." Rosecena opened it and saw everything was fine.

She wondered why there was a vase in the crate. "Everything's okay and I'm about to call mom right now." She hung up before he could warn her about the curse of the vase. Rosecena dialed the number, talked to a nurse and asked her to get her mother on the phone. "Dad is stuck in a tomb in Egypt and he could be hurt."

"Okay calm down! I'm going right now", mom said. Just take care of each other and your pets. Remind your sisters to do their exercises and make sure all of you guys do your homework, mom replied.

Rosecena replied, "Okay everything will be done, and Vickie and I will make sure the homework is done. Please take care of yourself and dad. Rosecena, you know how to cook so you are in charge of everything. You and your sisters take care of each other and the pets too. Oh, if there is a crate at the house. Don't let anything happen to it either. Don't worry, everything is fine", said Rosecena. After the call ended, Rosecena decided that they were going to eat pizza tonight, so she ordered for delivery to the house. Then, Rosecena went and finished cleaning up. She heard a lot of noises outside, so she went and checked to see what was going on.

When she opened the door, there stood a knight. Her sisters ran up behind her, and she told them to go and take their baths. They went and played X-Box video games instead. "Are you Rosecena Athlete?", he asked. "Maybe I am, maybe I'm not. I'm not telling you", she said. The knight replied, "I came to find Rosecena Athlete; if you are not her, I have to go."

"Okay, I'm Rosecena Athlete. Now what do you want with me." "I was sent here to protect you", he said. "What do you mean", Rosecena asked.

The knight replied, "The reason I'm saying that is because there is a monster that lives here, and I want you to destroy it so that the town stays safe forever." Okay, but you have to do what I say", said Rosecena. "No questions asked; just do what I ask of you or you will have to leave. Do you understand that? My sisters are the most important people here to me. I am glad that you want to help but know that if you put their lives in danger in any way, I will make you pay for that mistake in a very painful way." "Okay I understand that, said the knight and I will do whatever I can do to keep your sisters safe. I hope that you will live forever and your family too", the knight said.

This castle had a very cruel king living here during the eighteenth century. Everyone seemed to dislike him and wanted to try to find a way to kill him. Rosecena interrupted, "How does this involve me and my family?" The knight continued, "We left the monster in the castle hoping that no one would ever want to live here. Then your family moved in. The village feared that the monster would grow even bigger and then try to eat us." " What am I supposed to do?, she asked. I heard that you have killed many monsters, so we were hoping you could help us get rid of this one."

"I will see about killing the monster but where would it be hiding? It could be anywhere in a castle", she told the knight. What does it look like? " I'm not sure, but I do know that it escaped from a crate, killed people, and that it's mean. It apparently grew really tall. That's all I can tell you because that's all I know. Would you want me to stay and help you just in case?" "No thanks, replied Rosecena, I think I can do a little research. If you want to, you could go protect my sisters. Okay but would you please keep me informed because I don't want you or your sisters hurt and since you don't know much about the monster's I would also like you to promise for your sisters and parents that you will be very careful .

Okay, now go and watch my sisters because I'm going to try to figure out what the monsters look like and soon or a later how to kill it also. I am planning on making everything work out like it is supposed to be. Then also keep my sisters safe. When this is done you guys keep away from any more creatures okay.

I will try and take care of the monsters before our parents even think about coming home. Otherwise, there will be plenty of trouble for everyone. Then suddenly Rosecena heard a wolf howling so loud that she had to close the door.

That scared all of her sisters so bad that they ran to find Rosecena. The wolf was trying to break in so Rosecena walked out and broke a pole to kill it. Then she went back to try to find the monster named Creepy. The monster crept passed Rosecena and broke the vase, so Rosecena ran and got her first look at it. Creepy looked like an octopus with a mosquitos face. It had scales like an alligator because of its eyes.

The monsters went for the vase. Creepy knocked it down and ate the brains and blood. Rosecena ran at it to try and kill it but creepy grew about three feet tall. The monster used its tentacles and caught her in mid-air. Rosecena was caught and the monster tried it's best to eat her.

The knight saw that and got very discouraged and started to doubt that she would be able to kill the monster but he wanted to watch and see if she could he thought that she was trying to figure out the monster still but she was shocked because the monster was stronger than she thought and now she was nervous because the monster had caught her in the air but she was very smart and very good at thinking on her feet. She then knew that she would figure it out and kill the monsters because she hadn't let any monsters beat her yet. The problem was how you take out a monster that you don't know anything about all she knew is that it was trying to eat her and she wasn't going to let that happen at all.

As the monster started to lower her into its mouth, she grabbed the monster fang and pulled it down. The monster started screaming in pain because it hurt itself. Rosecena hadn't plan on doing that but she was glad she did till the monster threw her up in the air and she landed in a wad of pink bubble gum she looked to see where the gum was coming from and it was Creepy she was bleeding and spitting up. Just as Rosecena was standing up and freeing herself from the gum a huge mass of it hit her and knocked her down.

She finally got back up and started searching for the monster but she was gone and the trail of chewing gum was too. Rosecena wondered where she went, and how she could disappear so quickly. She decided that she was going to make this vow to herself that she would find and destroy her. She headed to the kitchen too finish the dishes because she was waiting on the deliver guy to arrive when the doorbell rang and it was the delivery guy she called her sisters to come and eat and invited the knight to sit down and eat with them, but he said that he had to go because the town had to be told that they had a great protector with them.

When she went to try to go to sleep that night she couldn't sleep so she decided that she would get up and keep watch for Creepy. She knew that she had school but she couldn't sleep no matter what she tried. She went into the kitchen and cleaned it up. She was suddenly attacked from behind.

She knew she had to defend herself so she pushed back with her back legs and then turn around so quickly that she hit the monster in the head Creepy was stunned that Rosecena had reacted like that so she let out a terrible growl.

The monster pushed Rosecena into the counter and then grabbed at her with her tentacles, but Rosecena was ducking and trying to figure out a way to hurt the monster where it would let out a lot of that pink chewing gum. When she slipped and the tentacles caught her she was trapped and she didn't like it. That's when the knight returned to Rosecena's house he saw that she was caught and attacked he had manage to cut off two tentacles when it threw Rosecena in the air, the knight caught Rosecena and put her on the floor when a wave of the chewing gum hit them and knocked them back to the ground again. He then threw a sword to her and saw that the sword wasn't going to do any good because the monster had disappeared again.

Rosecena went to thanking the knight when he snapped at her asking what happened and snapping that if she wasn't more careful the monster was going to kill her and there was nothing he could do about it. Rosecena smooth him by telling him not to worry the monster just got a lucky shot and that the monster was going to die when she gets her chance. The knight suggest that she go and rest but Rosecena refused telling him that she couldn't sleep she had too much worries on her mind that she had to take care of before she could relax. He then asks her what are you planning on doing then.

I'm going to search for the monster again and if this sword kills this monster then I'm going to hang on to it till I kill the monster okay? She started searching the house but all of a sudden, she heard the alarm going off announcing that it was time for school. They got dressed and at eight o'clock they were at school acting like nothing was happening at their house. They went through school cool and collected until it was time to go home.

Then they grew fearful of the monster. Their fears were recognized when they got home. They found their pets lying dead. The girls cleaned up after the dead pets with tears in their eyes they hated the monster for killing their pets so they told Rosecena to kill the monster quickly and painfully.

Rosecena decided to go and search the basement because in most cases that's where monsters would be hiding, but when she turned on the light she saw that it was too dark and that she wasn't prepared this time like she was usually.

She reached into her book bag and grabbed a flashlight. She then went into the basement to go and search for the monster. Then suddenly she heard her sisters screaming and she ran upstairs and saw Creepy. She grabbed her sword and stabbed her over and over.

She stabbed the monster ten times before it let her sisters go. She was planning on destroying the monster right then and there but the monster suddenly dropped her sisters. She had to catch them so they wouldn't be injured. Creepy got away again.

She tried to follow Creepy after she helped her sisters but she had already vanished. Rosecena felt so helpless because she couldn't be in two places at once. She was aggravated because she so hoped to end it already. She could see that she was going to have to come up with a much better plan to get rid of the monster and to protect her sisters. She was also aggravated because Creepy almost ate her sisters.

Plus she was frustrated at the knight for not being there when she needed him to be, but now she was more determined to kill the monster that she was ready to ask her sisters to spend the night with a friend. The sisters had never spent the night away from each other, so this would be painful for them. That why when Tiger came and ask Rosecena what they were going to do Rosecena grew a little more aggravated at her because she didn't know what to do. She decided to let them weigh their options then she told them that they had to let her know which one they were going to do by screaming because she was going to hunt again.

None of the girls wanted to go but they were scared and they knew that they were putting their lives and their sister life in danger by staying but they were also afraid to leave her alone because they thought that the monster might have poison. What if she got stab and she couldn't get to the phone then she might die because she wasn't able to get to the phone and no one was there to help her so they didn't want to make the choice because they were scared on both cases. The girls then remember a bracelet they had order for their great great grandmother and decided that they would make Rosecena promise to wear it so that if she gets hurt someone would help her.

Her sisters then asks her what are you planning on doing then? When Tiger told Rosecena that she said okay to the bracelet but she didn't know what to say about having to make a choice about sending them off or not. That's why when Sam and Rose said that they were scared she told them to go and take their bath and pack enough for about two weeks, she called Aunt Melinda and told her that she needed a favor and asked if it would be alright if her sisters came and stay a while with her because she had a problem she had to handle and she didn't want them in danger. She told her all the details about what was going on except that the monster ate the pets and almost ate her sisters.

Then she said okay they could come and they both hung up. Tiger then came down and asked if Rosecena thought that this was a good idea they all leaving her alone with the monsters and going to stay somewhere. When Rosecena told them that it was Aunt Melinda house they were going to stay at they knew they were going to be safer then Rosecena would be. Her sisters all came downstairs and started to complain about having to leave her so she told them all to sit down on the couch then started explaining the reasons they had to go to Aunt Melinda was because she couldn't protect them from Creepy and fight her with them there.

Now go and get your suitcases we have to get you guy to the airport your plane leave in an hour that gives us enough time to get there and to get you all on the plane. They came back down with their suitcase they had tears in their eyes. Rosecena knew why they were crying but she knew that it couldn't be help either because if they stayed there with her she would get hurt trying to protect them and if they go she might be safer. She told them I know you guys are worried about me but think about how much safer you guys will be when this monster is dead and you can come back here plus we can go to parties and have fun again.

Now come on its all prepared all I got to do is put you guys on the plane and Aunt Melinda will be there waiting to pick you guys up. I am going to kill this evil creature soon and then I am going to be able to sleep again and do my exercises. She then drove them to the airport before they even thought about getting on the plane they ran to Rosecena and wrapped her in a big hug with tears in their eyes they told each other they love them and the other girls except Rosecena loaded the plane. She watched as the plane took off and flew out of view before getting in the car and driving home with tears in her eyes she cried all the way home but by the time she got home she was okay again there was no tears in her eyes she had her skin tone back to its regular color and now she was more determined to kill it.

When she got home Creepy attacked. She fought as hard as she could but it wasn't doing any good. Every second of the attack felt like hours. She had stabbed the monsters about fifteen times and the monsters had cut her three times once in the arm, another time in the back then her leg got cut. The monster started trying to escape but Rosecena was following as quickly as she could.

She was annoyed at herself that Creepy got away she thought there should have been no way in heck that she got away. She decided that she had better go and check out her wounds she checked all of them and then started searching for Creepy when she heard a knock on the door. She ran to see who it was when she opened the door there stood a friend she hadn't seen in years. Rosecena said not that I'm not glad to see you but what are you doing here?

Xena replied I came to see you and warn you about the monster name Creepy. Rosecena asked what you know about her. I know how to kill it said Xena. Tell me how please said Rosecena.

First, you must tie her eight legs up. Then you stab her in the head in till she become an egg again another way is to make sure she doesn't get any blood. Xena then left and Rosecena went back to searching for Creepy again. She check her sisters rooms, the two restrooms, her parents room, the guest bedroom, basement, the attic, the maid rooms, the knights room, the musicians rooms, plus even her room. She was about to check the dungeon she was happy to know how to kill Creepy so she started to head downstairs, when she reminded herself that she owe Xena a thank you next time I see her. As she started down stairs into the dungeon the phone started ringing. She ran to the phone and answered it. It was her sisters; they were calling to see if they could come home yet. When Rosecena told them that she was about to kill the monster they rejoiced in happiness.

Then Rosecena went to the dungeon and found her. She got worried how am I supposed to tangle up her legs. She then came up with a wonderful plan. She started right away by getting her legs tangled in some rope she found in a box, she stabbed it in the foot. Then started running around the dungeon when the monster took a step she fell down. After it fell down and Rosecena stabbed the monster three times the monster became smaller.

The monster then ran away so weakened by now it wasn't even the size of a flee. Rosecena tried to catch the monster but it was too small and it escaped. Rosecena then heard the phone ringing and ran upstairs to see who was calling. It was her mom wanting to know how everything was going. Rosecena told her that everything was great.

She was hoping that everything would be okay but she also was mad that the monster got away yet again. She knew that she could kill it but if it gets too small it would escape. She knew that she would have a hard time now that she saw that happened, and then she promised herself one way or another next time she was going to catch it or make it become an egg before going anywhere else that way the monster wouldn't escape and she could be happy that the monster was finally dead. She started dancing from the happiness in her heart but then she remembers that the monster wasn't dead yet, so she didn't have a reason to celebrate yet. She promises herself soon the monster would be dead then she could go to having fun and training again. She missed her training because it always made her feel so strong when she trained.

Her mother informed her that they wouldn't be back for four weeks. Okay everything is fine here. I'm keeping the house super clean plus I've been trying to make sure that all the pets are feed and water before we go to school and then after we all feed the animals again. Then I make them train and do what they are supposed to be doing. Then I make them go get a bath. Then we finish all the homework and eat. After they finished talking she went back to trying to locate Creepy. The monster hid for about two weeks and then her sisters came home.

They asked her if the monster was dead and she answered her by saying that she didn't know. At least I know how to kill her now. Go upstairs and work on your homework, Rosecena said. They went upstairs while Rosecena left to check for the monster. Then she heard screaming. She ran to the source of the sound and found Creepy. She grabbed Creepy and then stabbed it, it became smaller. She stabbed it again and the monster turned into an egg." What in the world," said Rosecena?

At the same time her sisters asked, " What ? Rosecena showed them the egg. Then she called the knight. She looked at, where the broken vase was and saw it was fixed, on the counter. They saw all their pets were alive again.

She was so proud that the monster was finally died that she went and found her favorite punching bag and knocked the fire out of it then she kicked it a couple of times then she ran the track and just enjoyed a little bit of training while she was able to because she knew that once she was done she needed to go and help her sisters with their homework and then also feed all the pets, lock them up all up for the night and also take a bath, clean the house. Plus maybe get a great night of sleep since she hadn't slept in about four nights. She wanted to go and have fun the most though.

She felt like she wanted a good amount of fun for once and she wanted it to be with her sisters since they had been away from each other for two weeks, and they hated being away from each other more than anything in the world.

They were glad to be back together in the house that when Rosecena had finished her training she went straight up there and started to help with their homework when she saw that it was done, she asked them what they wanted to eat she had placed the egg in the crate and was hoping that the egg would never hatched again because the monster was such a pain in the butt, they wanted pizza so she called Pizza Hut got them to deliver and they enjoyed the pizza. After their pizza they played games for about fifteen minutes and then Rosecena told them to go and get ready for bed. The knight then arrived and he explained to them the reason their pets came back alive. Here is what he said from the beginning to the end: we got tired of being beat by a cruel king, so I sent Fred after a crate that had a monster's egg in it. Fred made sure the egg was sent to the king, and when the king saw the egg instead of gold.

He got really mad. He ordered the miners death. We waited for the monster to do the job. It killed the king, and we gave the monster the castle so that she wouldn't eat us. Then your dad came to the kingdom and we believed that the monster was dead, so we sold the castle to him.

We wouldn't have sold it to him if we had known the monster was still alive. We wouldn't have let him put his family in such grave danger. We believed that Creepy was dead. That's when we heard that your father found the lost tomb of Alexander the Great. He was the only king that we liked so much we had him buried with blood and guts. We believed that would bring Creepy back to life and we grew fearful for your family's life and the city. Then we heard about you.

I had to wonder if you could kill the monster, but I wouldn't get too hopeful. I heard many stories showing that you were a good killer for monsters but I didn't know if you were going to be able to handle this one because they say that this monster could get really tall. I never saw it through and I didn't want to see it tall either because they say that if it get tall you will be it next meal and I didn't want to be its next meal. I didn't even want to see the monster even one time.

Everyone told me that you could do it in no time. I was waiting to see you take it out and then when I saw you sending your sisters away. I was wondering if you were going to go with them or not if you went with them I was going to take that as a sign that you couldn't handle the monster and that I needed to go and kill the monsters. I didn't know how but when you stayed and started to head back to the castle I knew that you were either brave or stupid please forgive me for doubting you.

I didn't believe it after you got caught and hurt. Then Xena told us about you, we believed you could take care of the monster. You really proved to me that you can beat the odds. Did you know that your father is now our king?

You are our hero and I'm really glad you took care of the monster. Thank you Rosecena. You have saved us from a horrible monster and we owe you so much. You are stronger than you look said the knight.

Do you know how to take care of the egg and how to keep it from hatching again? The knights asked. No, said Rosecena I thought that it was taken care of already. When will it hatch again? How do you take care of it forever?

I don't know said the knight. That's when they heard a loud crash in the front room. They ran in and saw the shell of the egg. Rosecena's cat had knocked it off, the monster ate the cat and then it disappeared. The knight and Rosecena were shocked. How did the cat get the egg out of the crate and knocked it to the ground.

Rosecena was mad that the monster was back alive and now she was going to have to kill the monster again. Without getting hurt and protect her sisters the good thing was that the knight was there to help her now. She began to searched for the monsters but then she decided that she should ask her sisters to go stay somewhere else for the night but then decided against it, so while her sisters were in the house.

She decided to go and search for the monster without telling her sisters that they need to get out of the house. She then heard screaming in their bedroom and she ran upstairs and saw Creepy upstairs eating their pets. She grabbed her sword but then saw that Creepy had disappeared again. She then ran around the castle till she found her sisters. They were upstairs taking a bath.

She checked the bathroom to make sure that Creepy wasn't in there. Then she told her sisters what had happened. She then went down to the dungeon and stabbed Creepy. The knight was keeping Rosecena's sisters safe. She caught the monsters and put it in the crate and stabbed the monster again. After it became an egg she put it back in the crate and closed it up, she then nailed it thinking that it would definitely keep the egg safe from getting broke. She walked back to the knight and her sisters and told them that the egg is safely locked in the crate.

They went in to see the crate and that was when they see it totally destroyed what happened, they cried at the same time. How can this be, Rosecena screamed. This is the second time, I have caught the monster and it escaped. How and why?

She was frustrated but she was going to make sure that she got the monster again and then lock it up where it couldn't get away one way or another. She now knew that the monster could break free from crates and that's was something that she did need to find out so that it wouldn't happened again. She then decided to go and search for the monster but she headed upstairs and saw the monsters trying to eat her pets again, but she wouldn't let her eat her pets again without thinking she grabbed the monster and stabbed the monster with her own tentacles. The monsters started to bleed the pink chewing gum when Rosecena heard the doorbell ringing she didn't want to go and answer it but when she turned back the monster was gone and so was the trail of pink chewing gum.

She was frustrated because of the monster getting away again. She went to check the door but no one was there. She then went and checked on her sisters and she knew that the monsters needing to be killed. She was also determined that the monster was going to be killed soon the castle would be monster free.

She went to her room and started to pray that somehow she would get the answer on how to kill this monster before anyone get hurt and that it wouldn't come back after she kill it this time. She was hoping that she could use the same trick as she used earlier but then she was thinking that the monster might have learned how to defend itself from that trick. She also knew that she had to believe that she could kill the monster but she was worried that the monster was going to end up killing her.

Then she heard the door bell ringing again she ran downstairs and answered the door. It was Xena she was there to give her some new advice about the monster. Xena told her that she had to freeze the egg but you must be prepared for a fight. "Why," asked Rosecena? Isn't it at its weakest when it's an egg? Yes unless you make it turn into an egg two times or more.

Rosecena turned to say thank you but she had already left. Rosecena walked over to her sisters and asked them to help her come up with a plan. She informed them with what she knew already. They had a difficult time coming up with a plan.

Rosecena decided to ask them to help her so she went and told them what she had learned. She then asked them if they were hungry. They started to head downstairs Rosecena was in the lead and Creepy attacked her. Rosecena was fighting with all of her might but it wasn't doing any good the monster had escaped again and she had no idea where to find her.

She knew about the freezer downstairs in the dungeon and upstairs in the kitchen. The problem was how to get the monster in there and how to turn the monster back into the egg. She didn't know much about the monster, so she didn't know what to expect or how to get control over it. She also didn't know it had mind control over the knight.

She wanted the monster dead more now more than ever. It had hurt her by one of its tentacles. She knew that the monster would attack again but she didn't know how or when. She wanted her sisters to either be in bed or outside before the monsters even thought about attacking them again. She was glad that the monster attack her most of the time and not her sisters. She thought that if the monster attacked her sisters that it would either hurt them or even worst.

That's night while Rosecena was fixing dinner, and then someone knocked at the door. Her sister Tiger ran to the door and answered it, there stood a knight he said that his name was David. I've come to help Rosecena if I can. Where would I locate her?

Tiger showed him the way to the kitchen where Rosecena was cooking dinner. David introduced himself and then he asked if he could stay with them to help. He told her about the discussing the matter with all the other knights. She said I've been trying for a long time to kill the monster. What are you going to do? You must protect your sisters and you need help because you can't kill the monster and protect your sisters.

Please allow me to help you so that you can have one less worry while you hunt for the monster. How I would have to protect you from the monster also, Rosecena asked. Just then Creepy attacked again. This time David stabbed the monster and it ran away.

Okay, you can stay said Rosecena, but you must protect my sisters or you deal with me, understood? She finished supper and they ate. David then exclaimed that was some good cooking. They talked together for about an hour and then she decided that it was time to go and hunt for the monsters she started in the attic then worked her way down.

When she got to the dungeon she still couldn't find the monster. She grew aggravated and then went upstairs to where her sisters and the knights were and was still trying to figure out what to do. She knew that the monsters could freeze but like Xena said be ready for a fight. It would be aggravating if she got hurt while trying not to freeze to death herself. She didn't want her sisters in the house when she even thought about fighting the monster again.

She told them that her plan was to freeze the monster. She was going to open the freezer in both the kitchen and the dungeon and turn on the air conditioners to below freezing levels. She was hoping that the monster would get to cold and then the monster would attack her to warm up. She told them that they would have to make some choices and be very careful.

Creepy should definitely freeze and really fast, so I should be able to stab her a few times so it will turn into an egg again, hopefully a frozen one. What if it don't work, asked Tiger. I will figure out away, believe me.

What if you get hurt or killed and Creepy gets out of the house, asked Sam. Then everyone is in extreme danger, said Rosecena. Let's hope for the best, said Rosecena. Do the five of you want to go out or stay in because it will be really cold, said Rosecena? It's up to you, said her sisters. Do you guys want to go and watch a movie or stay here and freeze. I won't be able to keep you safe while I am trying to kill Creepy and keep myself safe too. We want to go to a movie, said the sisters. They left and Rosecena started to work on her plan.

She was going to locked up the house where no one could get in or out without her knowing about it first. She was also planning to be really cold and she didn't really like that but she would do what she could to protect her sisters without seeing any of them get hurt. Plus she didn't want herself to get hurt, even protect the villages and the rest of the world too. She didn't want anyone hurt either and she didn't want to be alone either.

She went to the control panel and turned it to freezing, she opened both freezers. Then she heard a growl. It looks like I'm making Creepy very mad, she told herself. Rosecena knew that she would get cold so she hurried up and changed into warmer clothes. That's when she heard another growl.

She went to investigate it and there was the first knight. She saw that the knight was helping Creepy by turning off the air conditioner, so she attacked the knight and the knight fought back. She then knocked him out. Rosecena helped him come out of the mind control and then also helped him up.

She asked him what his problem was. Somehow the monster was controlling me, he said. Rosecena went to the control box and turn it to even colder. Then she took the knight home and asked the others knight to keep him there.

When she got home she saw the monster and it attacked severely. When she was finished the monster became an egg and it was frozen solid, so she took the egg to the dungeon and locked it up with chains on the door handle. She turned up the heat to warm up and closed the freezer in the kitchen.

While she warmed up the house she was waiting for the house to warm up because she was even colder than ever. She then decided that she had better start cleaning the house. She was so cold that she was shivering badly. She knew that her mother would be very mad if she walked in and saw the house like it was, so she was trying to fight through her being so cold while trying to clean up.

She then heard a knock on the door and she knew that it was time for her to go and check and see who that was. She was also hoping that it would warm her up. She didn't like that no one even knew much about the monster. She was strong yeah but she didn't think that she was that strong.

When her sister's got home with David, they decided to help Rosecena clean up while she was taking her bath. She needed to warm up and a hot bath would do the trick. They then asked, Rosecena to tell them what happened. I will but first let's get the house in order. Why? When are mom and dad coming home?

I don't know that's why I am saying that it could be soon though, said Rosecena. They got it cleaned back up and then the sisters asked her to tell them again. She went upstairs and David followed because he wanted to know too.

When she was finished telling them they could hardly believe how one of the knights was being controlled by the monster. They were amazed that their sister was so brave. They were thrilled that Creepy would no longer be around. They were thankful their sister was strong and the fact that she was still alive was a blessing and they hoped the monster would stay frozen solid. They were glad that the monster might never be back ever again.

David and Rosecena walked back downstairs. She felt confident her sisters would rest tonight no matter what. David took his helmet off and she saw his handsome face for the first time. David liked her and Rosecena liked him so much.

David was extremely kind to her and her sisters. When she needed something he helped. David asked Rosecena if she was seeing anyone. After she said no he asked her to be his girlfriend.

Then she started to get worried because she was worried that if any of the monsters got freed then people might get hurt and that was a price she was worried about. The good news that for the moment nothing could happen because the monster was no longer where it could move without her knowing about it first.

They kept watch to make sure Creepy never got out again and he tried to keep his girlfriend safe. Rosecena also wanted to protect him and her family. They wanted to keep their town monster free. She was excited that all their pets were back alive and none of them was going to die if she had her way.

When their parents came home it was Christmas. They decorated for Christmas and were so excited their parents got back in time. They had bought their parents gifts. When they see their gifts they said, we need to go shopping, having already in minded what to get their girls.

When they arrived home they wrapped the girl's gifts and placed them under the tree. Then waited for them to wake up while enjoying their hot chocolate. They ran downstairs and excitably opening their gifts they received. They were really happy when they found out they received everything they wanted and more.

They gave their parents lots of hugs. They were all very happy. Then their dad noticed that the vase wasn't broken, and then asked how have you managed to keep it so clean around here? Considering that the monster was around and about. He said to Rosecena, Listen, I am the son of King Chris and when he started to beat everyone the guards took me away from my father for my protection.

He was so proud that for the first time he could tell his daughters and that for the first time he could tell everyone the truth. Plus for the first time he could brag on his daughter and on himself. He then told them everything he could so that he could get it all off of his chest and he was very glad of that.

They told me what would happen so I left. They took me to Louisiana, and then after he died I had to find a bride and return as the king. I did as I was told. I fell deeply in love with your mom and asked her for her hand in marriage.

We didn't know we would have such independent daughters that can look out for each other. Your mom dreamed of having a slayer. I also didn't know that she would have a gymnastic champion and a vet that would be the best ever. You have made us so pleased for being so determined on keeping the town safe.

Thanks.

Why didn't you tell us there was a monster here? How could you keep that from us? Were you trying to protect us? We were bound to find out but why did I have to from my friend.

What if I hadn't been able to take care of the monster? Then what would have happened? What if I couldn't protect my sisters from Creepy then what would happen? I know you could take care of the monster.

She knew that it wasn't going to be easy to get her father to see that he was wrong for not just telling her about the place where they were going to be living for the rest of their life but she was really good at getting her dad to do what she wanted to do. She knew that she would get her dad to say what she wanted before sundown so she didn't even worry about rather or not to be too mad at him or not. She also was going to get her mother to say sorry too because she could have warned her too and to put her sisters in a safe place too.

We put all our faith in you. I knew that you had the strength and the courage to take care of everything. I knew you would be left in charge and you would be the one to beat the monster. Then someone knocked on the door. Troy answered the door. There stood an old lady. She asked him if he could give her the location of Rosecena Athlete. I need her help. It's an emergency. Her dad called Rosecena to the door.

The lady said that there was a huge monster she needed help with. She told her how she had traveled from Washington to where she was now. She told her how at nighttime a huge wolf would attack their village and how every night would break into someone's house and try to harm them. She asked Rosecena, can you help?

Her dad said go on and take care of the monster and then come back home and open your gifts except I'd like you to open this one now. It will help you take care of yourself. Please try not to get hurt. When you get back we will talk, as I have so much to talk to you about. Okay, said Rosecena. I'll see you guys later. I will miss you all so much.

They left and then Rosecena went to Washington to kill the monster. She had to fight a huge werewolf but she didn't really mind because she got to learn how to fight werewolves. She knew how to kill werewolves she now knew that to kill werewolves you either use a gun with silver bullets or to hit them in the head with something silver in the head hard enough to kill the monsters. She didn't have much trouble with the monster but she always killed any monsters when she gets the chance.

She killed the monster and then headed home. When she arrived home she went straight to check on the egg, when she couldn't find the egg she grew very worried that the monster would break free and try to kill everyone. She decided to go and ask her mother if she knew where the egg was and when her mother said yes she asked her where it was? Her mother said in your room I thought that you might want to save it for remembrances. I hope that it didn't hatch because if it did we have a huge problem to deal with.

Rosecena ran to her room and found Creepy. The monster ran off before she could get close. She ran down to where her family was and told them that they had a problem and that they could either call the knights or stay at Aunt Melinda's. Please take the pets so Creepy won't devour them. I must freeze Creepy again.

I'm sorry, Rosecena I didn't mean to free the monster, I'm really sorry.

Would you please forgive me? Don't worry, mom. I already forgave you and I love you, said Rosecena. I killed the monster once already. I can and will do it again. I need all of you to leave for just a little while so I can freeze it again. Thanks.

They all left and Rosecena then turned the air conditioner to freezing. She opened the freezer door in the kitchen and the dungeon and locked all of the doors. She heard the fiercest growl that told her she would probably have to fight with every ounce of her strength. Her knight boyfriend tried to help but didn't succeed. Rosecena screamed when Creepy huge tentacle pierced him and then he fell to the floor Rosecena ran to him and try to keep pressure on his wound so he might survive, but he didn't survive. Rosecena was so mad she went and turned on the air condition in the attic. She then heard an even louder growl and she knew that the monster was getting even madder because it was getting really cold. She then walked to the kitchen and started to wait for the monster to attack she was also hoping that she would warm up soon.

Rosecena was really cold but she knew that soon enough that she would be warm up because the monster would be back in the egg again. She went to her bedroom and put on more warm clothes trying to get warm again because she wasn't happy at all. She patiently waited for the monster to attack her so that she could make sure it became the egg again, but the monster wouldn't attack her like she was wanting.

By the time the monster growled again. Rosecena got busy tracking it and came very close to it when the phone rang. She answered and her mom said, have you taken care of the monster yet? No but don't worry.

All I have to do is let it get colder in here, and then you can say goodbye monster when it tries to attack me. Keep me informed please and take care. I will start Rosecena and I want to believe this monster is going down. It got really cold and the monster attacked again.

Rosecena fought as hard as she could but Creepy ended up hurting her she was bleeding in her stomach and back and felt a stinging sensation. She didn't know how bad she was hurt. She bandaged herself up and fought the painful sensation. Then she took off again to locate Creepy.

She made it so cold she was just about to freeze herself. She finally found Creepy and the battle began again. Then all of a sudden Creepy disappeared. How did that happen she wondered?

She called the knights and asked them if they knew that the monster could disappear. When they said they didn't know. She then went outside to get a breathe because the poison was taking a lot of energy from her. When she came back in she was still trying to get her energy back but she knew that she would make the monster pay and try to remember to thank everyone who had helped her. She then went searching again and couldn't find Creepy. She searched every room and see even went to make sure that the freezers was getting cold enough that she was hoping that the monster would freeze solid too. She was warm but she about had it with the monster and the poison and pain that she was going through.

Then someone knocked at the door. She unlocked the door and let Xena in. She told her that she must make it colder. She said okay and told her thanks. She ran and turned on all of the air conditioners. It became so cold Creepy could not disappear again. She fought again but Creepy got away. Then she came upon a nest of eggs.

The monster had seven eggs all different colors. The first one was pink with purple spots. The second purple with blue spots. The third yellow with white spots. The fourth green with pink spots. The fifth black with white spots. Then blue with orange, then brown with white spots. She took them to the freezer. She caught Creepy and tied up its legs so she could stab it.

Yes, she said then took the egg to the freezer and bolted the door. She called her mom and told her she had taken care of Creepy, thanks goodness she said. Now warm up the house, we'll be there shortly. When they got home they wanted to know everything.

Then she called the knights over. Why haven't you tried to protect us, she asked? I had to take care of the monster myself. Twice I have saved the city. I could have used some help you know.

Rosecena was annoyed but she wasn't worried anymore because now the monster was locked up and if Rosecena got her way the monster wasn't getting out again. She then decided that she wanted a way to lock all of the monsters away from the rest of the family so that the monsters couldn't get away again.

She then had to go back down stairs and try to warm up because she was still really cold. The knight ran off to tell everyone the monster was dead and that they could now return back to the castle. They didn't know about the eggs that Rosecena had hidden in a cold location. The knights and the maids went back to the castle to do their jobs. They were very pleased that the monster's was gone.

That night a maid took out some eggs to make a cake. She then walked away from the counter. When she turned back around she discovered the eggs broken. Rosecena then came into the kitchen and saw the eggs out she then asked who took the eggs out and why?

The maid then told Rosecena that she did and she was so sorry, she wanted to explain why she took the eggs out but Rosecena told her that they didn't have time for any explanations right now. She could explain everything after the monster was dead again. The maid then told everyone that they must get out that their lives were in grave danger. Everyone left the castle except this little girl name Cameron Elizabeth.

Rosecena turned on the air conditioners and opened the freezers doors in both the kitchen and the dungeon. It was so cold that it caused the monsters to attack at the same time. Rosecena fought as hard as she could but it was a great conflict out of control. Cameron Elizabeth was screaming and trying to scare some of them away.

When it didn't work she began to fight also. Rosecena had five fighting her and Cameron had two fighting her. The two girls fought with every ounce of strength they had. They were getting really tired when the monsters saw that they started attacking even harder.

They started working their way to the freezer hoping that the monster would follow them and then they could lock them up but that was a wish that wouldn't happened. Unfortunately none of it worked and that made them very unhappy. The monster then ran off leaving the girls to try and plan another assault on the monsters. The girls tried to follow the monsters but some of the monsters turned and attack leaving about fifteen of the monsters fighting the girls.

The girls didn't give up fighting they thought that they were beating the monsters when suddenly they disappear. This might be more difficult than I had imagined Rosecena told Cameron you might consider leaving the castle for your safety. Cameron surprised Rosecena by saying that she wanted to stay and help her right now because she didn't want to leave her at a time when there was so much to do and not enough people to help anyone. The girls then teamed up and started working together when they heard the phone ringing it was Xena.

She was calling to make sure that their hero was still alive. Xena decided that she wanted to know what to do: should she come over or stay at her house. Rosecena said that it was up to her but she has got to be careful if she comes over. Xena then came over to Rosecena's house and asked how could she help?

Xena arrived and asked what did they want her to do? Rosecena explained that Creepy had babies so we need to come up with an outstanding plan. They had already tried just about everything. They agreed to make it even colder than ever.

Then they heard another loud growl and they knew that it was Creepy and her babies. Cameron then asked what we do if they attack us again. You guys will make sure that the monsters attack me and then push me into the freezer and close the door. When I knock three time let me out that will be how we know that it is safe to let me out. I will be really cold but I will also be cleaning the house when I get out of the fridge.

Hopefully this plan will work you guys are to hide and get the monsters to attack me only ok? What if it doesn't work what if the monster sees your plan and run off before it works? If it comes to that then I will get you guys out and freeze the whole house. They did as they were told.

Only this time it was forty monsters. They came at Rosecena with all they had but soon caught on to their plan and ran away. When they knew they were being defeated, they ended up freezing around twenty of them. The girls asked Rosecena, how come there were so many monsters. How did that come about?

Something else that was amazing was no one known about Cameron's secret. She had special powers, she could elevate objects from a distances. She also had super speed and was very good at any and all sports. She also could control the weather. She always thanks God for her gifts because she was so proud of them.

I beat that that gift will come in handy today she thought and she went and checks the temperature. It was just right for the monsters to be cold. The monsters then decided to attack again, but instead of twenty it was fifty. Oh no, how can I defeat this many thought the girls to their self.

When the monsters attack all three of the girls Rosecena then stabbed the others monster to detracted the monsters from the other girls and make them attack her then the girls pushed Rosecena and all but ten monsters into the fridge and lock the monsters in the fridge with Rosecena after about ten minutes of hard hits on the door by the monsters Rosecena knocked three times and they let out a freezing Rosecena. She was shivering and she was breathing really hard. The monsters had taken a lot of energy from her but she was happy that she had frozen that many monsters with the help of her friends.

That's when Xena told Rosecena that ten had got away. They felt lucky that they got rid of fifty, but she was kind of annoyed that ten got away. They then heard the phone ringing again, Rosecena ran to go and answer it and found out that it was her mom. Then she explains what was going on and her mom asked what if we bring in more refrigerators.

That sounds great mom. They all hooked up the fridges and it got really cold even colder than before. After the girls got all of the fridges hooked up the monsters attacked again and they pushed Rosecena and the last ten into the fridge and when they finally heard the three knocks that Rosecena told them to wait for they breathe a sigh of relief. They all screamed out Hallelujah! All the monsters are finally died.

They closed all the fridges and turned off the air conditioners so that the house would warm up again, when Cameron said hey let's take a break I know this place where we can have a lot of fun and get something to eat. They headed downtown to a store called Twilight. It had everything you could ever see at a store.

Rosecena noticed a bookstand while the others were browsing about. She saw a book called monster world. She briefly read it and decided that she needed this book. Then they came to Rosecena and asked if she was hunger when she said yes they all went and ate a nice meal.

They got to meet a lot of wonderful waitresses their names was Alice, Elena, and Mamma. They were so nice and gave them a tour of the huge store. The girls hung out for a while and made friends. The owner of the store gave Rosecena the Monster World book. After they enjoy their meal they all went home Rosecena got home and started cleaning up the pools of water.

She finally got the house clean and started reading the book. What was fascinating was a monster called Kricketia. It fascinated her so much that she had to read some more to find out more. She kept reading; there were forty nine pages about the Kricketia.

Here is some of the stuff she read: the monster gets up to sixty to eighty feet tall, and has poison when it becomes small. The second time it can use its poison over and over again. Watch out and make sure you don't get stabbed by the monster tentacles then you will be poisoned. She kept reading.

It also has mind control and can fly. It learns while you're fighting it, so you have to try out different fighting skills. It opens its wings at different times. It's hard to get control over it.

It fears thought is fire. It can catch on fire but it doesn't kill it. You must watch out for its eyes because that's how it will control you. SO BEWARE!!!

It can only be frozen by ice. It has to be frozen over the monster not the egg. Then it will start to shrink. That made Rosecena really upset because she was hoping that the monsters was going to be frozen for a long time now she knew what she had to do but to do it was a whole different story.

The book had all the answers she needed but it was easier said than done. She went down to the living room and told her father and her mother the news. They asked her what was she going to do and she told them that she was going to have to try again. They left without any arguing knowing that she was scared and didn't want them hurt.

After they all left Rosecena went to the refrigerators and started to pull out the eggs while she was doing that she was breaking the eggs. It didn't take long for the monsters to run away and for her to know that she was all along this time and that she had to be careful because if she got stabbed it could be the end of her life forever. She was also glad that she was alone because the monsters was poisonous this time so if any one got hurt and die she would never forgive herself. She thought of that while she was waiting for all of the monsters to get far enough and not know what she was about to do.

The monsters ran away and then when they were gone she'd turned the air to freezing. It made her shiver. The monsters became cold and started shrinking. They quickly became ice. Thanks goodness, she said.

Then she forced them with all her strength into the freezers. I've got to get warm so she warmed up the house. She called her family and said it's finished. You can come home now.

Upon arriving home their mother noticed that Rosecena was shivering and said, you need a hot bath. Go ahead and we will clean the house and fix you dinner. You've done a great job and we're proud of you. When Rosecena came back down stairs she had stopped shivering and felt a lot better.

They then inquired to what happened. She explained everything and how the Monster World Book inspired her to put her plan to action. Then she enjoyed the wonderful meal with them and their company lifted her spirits up. This is what she needed.

To relax in her family presents was so joyful and no monsters: so she thought. She was very glad that the monsters were all gone. She didn't want to have to deal with any more monsters but she will have to soon or a later. The family was going to make the most of the peace and quiet thanks to the monsters being dead.

Everyone was happy and the other returns back to the castle. The girls went to the movies and enjoy the movie while the girls were relaxing their mother and father was just relaxing and watching TV. The girls then started to head home when they were jumped by seven strangers the guys thought that they were going to rob the girls and take everything from them.

The guys had the girls surrounded and started to come even closer to them trying to take their money and to hurt them the guys didn't know what was about to happen to make them regret surrounding them and trying to steal their money.

Rosecena would never let anyone steal from her or her family. When the guys try to grab Rosecena's bag she slap their hand and told them not to touch the bag or her sisters again or they won't like what happens next. The guys grabbed for Tiger's bag and Rosecena just kick one of the guys so badly that he hit the brick wall and left a dent in it.

Now do you believe me? If I was you guys I would leave before I decide to make you pay for your horrible actions. One of the guys then said so you got a tough kick lucky shot for you but you won't get another one. That's what you think just then he grab for Rosecena hand and he hit the wall just like the other guy did but when he moved again he saw that his head was bleeding and he really couldn't believe that he got hurt by a girl that's made him really mad he rushed at Rosecena and she did a round house kick and he fell down bleeding more.

This is the last time I'm warning you if you even think about attacking me and my sisters again I will get some cops to get you and your horrible friends now go away or I can keep letting you hurt yourself. One of his friends then try to grab Rose but Rosecena noticed and got him away from her sisters before he even touch her. She wished that they would just take the hint and leave but for some reason they kept coming and trying to attack. That's when they heard a loud hissing noise.

That made everyone turns around and looks for the source it really freaked everyone out when they saw a guy standing there with fangs hanging out of his mouth, then he spoke to the thieves you guys have ten seconds to drop whatever you have taken from those nice ladies before you wish that you weren't born and I mean now! They gave back what they had taken which was just a shirt and then ran off. The guy then jumps down and started walking towards them. Rosecena then step in front of him and said thanks but is there something that I could do for you.

He then said No I just wanted to make sure you guys was ok. Yeah thanks then she introduced her family to him and she found out that his name was Ron. Thanks for your help she said then he asked can I give you and your sisters a ride home. Yes thank you she wanted to find out more about him right now all she knew was she had to get her sister's home they were totally freaked out.

They then got to their house and she told her sisters to go ahead inside that she wanted to talk to Ron a little while longer. They went inside and left Rosecena to talk to Ron a little bit longer. Rosecena knew that he was a vampire because she heard him hissing and she knew that it was him. Plus she saw his fangs they were really white but she knew that he wasn't going to try and hurt her because he would have already tried.

When she asked him if maybe they could hang out some more tomorrow and he said no. Okay thanks anyway for saving us and she went to getting out when he grab her hand and said please be careful there are dangers in there that you will never imagine. I will and thank you for caring. Plus I know you are a slayer, I know that you are nice only to good vampires.

I was hoping that next time you have any dangerous creatures to battle you will call me and let me help you with it. Oh okay I will but only because you are a vampire and there should be no way that you get killed by a monsters. You can be killed by me but not a monster that I have already killed. She then went into the house before he could stop her again.

He wanted to tell her that in that castle there are still some monsters but he couldn't stop her in time to warn her. He knew that she could handle it but he didn't want to leave her unprotected either. It really shocked him how tough she was because the last time he fought a slayer was when he was first bitten and that was over two hundred years ago. He had killed the slayer with no problem but now he wouldn't even think about ever hurting a slayer.

She thought he was hot but he didn't like her because she was a slayer and he knew that it was never a good idea to even think about dating a slayer because usually someone gets killed and it usually the vampire that gets killed.

That's one reason he hated slayers but he didn't want her hurt either. He decided that to make sure that she didn't get hurt and he didn't get killed he would keep an eye on her that way if there was any more monsters she would be safe and so there wouldn't be a meaner slayer to have to deal with.

She spoke to soon. The monsters had made more babies but it wasn't just the one that was weak against ice the mate was weak against fire and the correct name for it monster type was an Aradobbles. It is the other kind that died by fire, and unfortunately it, made a new type that Rosecena would have to figure out and add information about because no one had ever seen this type. She was shocked by seeing the Aradobbles. Rosecena was going to have to figure out two different monsters and protect her family from the monsters.

All of the monsters started to grow, even the iced ones. I guess because she was eating the fire ones. All but around fifty five escaped. These were fast and could climb walls not as weak as the others. She asked her family to go out of the house again for a while. Meanwhile they got bigger and meaner. The monsters freed their family. They were hungry so they feasted on the pets this made them even bigger. Rosecena grew very angry at the monsters for eating her pets, so she attacked them again. She knew that she was poison but she was going to make the monsters paid for everything eating her family pets and killing her boyfriend and poisoning her. She only wished she knew how she could do that.

She was relaxing when she got home. When she got home her parents and sisters came to her and asked who that was? Rosecena started to explain who he was and what he was. Then she heard a loud knock on the front door.

When she answered the door there stood a huge wolf. She really didn't want to fight it but she would if she had to. She then started to close the door when the wolf suddenly talked. Are you Rosecena Athlete? He asked. Yes I am what can I do for you?

First you can get out of this house and let me kill this monster. Let me get this straight you have come to help me. Yes I did I know that there a monster in here that will kill any and all creatures that is here and even humans also. That's why I want you to leave this house and take your family too that way no one gets hurt and if I kill this monster and it's finally over we can all relax.

What if the monsters kill you then it will get bigger and I will have to kill meaner and bigger monsters that will be even meaner than before. Okay, maybe I do need to leave you to deal with these awful creatures but please call if you need any help either me or Ron my name is Andrew. Okay, I will are you telling me that there more monsters in here now?

Thanks anyway through it is nice to know that in this town everyone care so much. When I'm done with these creatures everyone who has offered to help me better be ready to go to the movies with me as a thank you presents ok. We will have to see about that okay. I hope that you don't die because if you do then we will have an even bigger problem.

After Andrew left the castle, Rosecena went into the castle again and saw that her family was gathering around talking and enjoying their selves. She really didn't want to ruin their joy but she really didn't want to have any of them hurt either so she went into the living room where all of her family was and asked her mother and father to come to the kitchen she needed their advice right away. She explained what she had learned to her parents and then asked them what they thought she needed to do.

They said that it might be the best to take everyone out and get them some relaxing they got Rosecena's sisters out of the house and then Rosecena knew that she could easily get rid of the Kricketia. She called the delivery truck and asked them to bring a bunch of ice-boxes and air-conditioners. When they arrived she asked them to help her set up all of them and then she told them that they needed to get out because it was about to get really cold and she was going to have a battle soon. She had completely forgot about Cameron Elizabeth offered to help with the monsters any time that she needed help. Rosecena was only worried about not letting the monsters get away or herself getting hurt. She turned on all of the air-conditions and the freezers and it started to become too cold for her so she went and got some long sleeves shirts on and her usual pants for fighting monsters.

Her plan for the Kricketia was really simple but she didn't want it to become complicated either. She was just going to make it too cold for the monsters and then push them into the freezer and lock up the Kricketia that all she had plan for the monsters at that moment and she would be happy just to get rid of even one of them at any time. Rosecena was waiting for the monsters to attack when she heard loud growling she was worried about the monsters all attacking if the Aradobbles attacked and the Kricketia then she most likely would not make it through it without being injured and that wouldn't be a good idea for her to be stabbed by any of the monsters. She was hoping that only the Kricketia would attack and then she could work on the Aradobbles.

When the Kricketia attacked and there was no Aradobbles she knew that she might be able to get some of them locked up but not all of them. She then started to fight the Kricketia so that she could lock them up but they started to run away she push nine of them in the freezers and knocked a few of them into the other freezers she was hoping that she would get all of the monsters either locked up or even died. She knew that a lot of the monsters had got a way so she knew that she was going to have to keep on trying to kill them when she suddenly remembered Cameron Elizabeth promised to help whenever she needed it so she called her and asked her if she had time to come and help her with these monsters that way they could have all the Kricketia died and she would be happy because she would be able to have some help with the dangers of being overwhelmed by all of the Kricketia attacking all at once. She was really fearful that might happened but she would handle it to the best of her abilities.

She had complete faith in her strength and her faith she knew that as long as she had both of those things she had nothing to fear. She was also worried that if she got hurt by the monster's tentacles. She really didn't want to be poison by the monsters and she was glad that soon the monsters would be died and she wasn't going to be alone just in case something happened and she got poisoned. When Cameron Elizabeth arrived at their castle she asked her what she could do to help just be ready to push me into the freezer with how ever many might attacked me ok.

I don't want you hurt so this is the best idea I can come up with so that you might not get hurt and hopefully I won't get hurt either. It was really cold and that made all of the Kricketia mad because they couldn't handle the cold at all. The two girls were really cold but they were determined to rid the castle of any and all of the monsters. Rosecena was just waiting for the monsters to attack her so she made it even colder they then heard the monster's loud growling again and she knew that they would soon attack them so she told Cameron to hide and when they attacked her to then to knocked her into the freezer hopeful they would all be on her and that would be the end of those monsters and they would just have to figure out the other monsters weakness.

They just had to wait for the monsters to attack her, when they did Rosecena nodded to Cameron to knock her into the freezer so that they would have frozen monsters. Cameron knocked her into the freezers and the monsters growled with such anger that it scared both of them and all the animals outside of the castle's wall, but soon the monsters was falling down weak they started to freeze but Rosecena didn't give the sign in till they were all frozen to death. It took about fifteen minutes by that time Rosecena was seating on the floor trying to fight the cold. She was starting to freeze to death so she knocked right when the last one had just frozen to death.

She was glad to get out of there but she was really ready for some warmth so that she could stop shivering, but she was not even going to allow herself to warm up till she get rid of all of the monsters that way she knew that it was safe and she could be happy again. She could start doing things with her family and maybe she could have a boyfriend one day. She had one but he had got stabbed by the Kricketia and had died. She hated all types of monsters because of that and she was determined that one day there would not be any monsters except the good monster.

She had to try and kill them, but she didn't know how. How do you kill these monsters she thought to herself? She went back to where her family was and told them that she had come across a monster that she was having a horrible time trying to kill. She asked her sisters to research all types of monsters to help her kill them. Xena called and told her Aradobbles weakness.

They all researched, but nothing coming up on the mix of two monsters. She now knew what the Aradobbles weakness was it was fire. She needed to find out the weakness of the new monster. Rosecena wanted to get rid of all the monsters, but the new monsters and the other monster was making it really hard.

Rosecena then decided on a plan, but she got scared and started to doubt thinking about its poison and possibly dying. She rebuked fear and encouraged herself, for she thought of many things in life she needed to do. She gained faith and was thinking of a plan when the doorbell rang. It was a woman named Martha.

She asked did they have a room for the night. I'm tired and need so desperately to rest, replied Martha. Rosecena replied you May not want to stay here because it is really dangerous. We have a monster running around and I don't know if I can protect you. If you decide to stay, I will do my best at protecting you.

Then Rosecena went to her family and talked to them about Martha staying the night. Her sister then suggest that they hang up nets to catch the monster and too protect them. She then went back to Martha to find out what her answer was and Martha had decided to stay. Rosecena then showed her to the room she was going to be staying in, but before Martha could go in Rosecena checked the room out, to make sure there were no monsters. She then suggested that if she got scared to go and stay in the same room as her family. Martha agreed and promised to do so.

Rosecena showed her around the castle and set up the cot near the family. Rosecena set up protecting nets everywhere that she could think of. She hired a cook to fix supper and then set off to locate the monster. She disregarded the cold plan on the count of so many people in the house. She didn't mind being cold when it is just her. She wouldn't let others be cold.

Rosecena thought of burning the Aradobbles kind to death. But she couldn't figure out about the others. She didn't know the fire method would work on them so she needed to think of something else. When they sat down for supper and she decided afterward to discuss her options with her family. They always try to help but Rosecena tries to cover them with protection.

They sat and started discussing what to do about the monsters. How could she get rid of all of them? They couldn't think of anything. They were growing irritated when someone knocked at the door. It was a strange guy who only said to burn the Aradobbles and on the other ones to do testing then he ran off.

She started to search the house for the Aradobbles but instead she found a big room where it was a huge stove. Now if she could lock all of the Aradobbles in there without having to lock herself in there with them it would be for the best. She knew that but she was also more worried

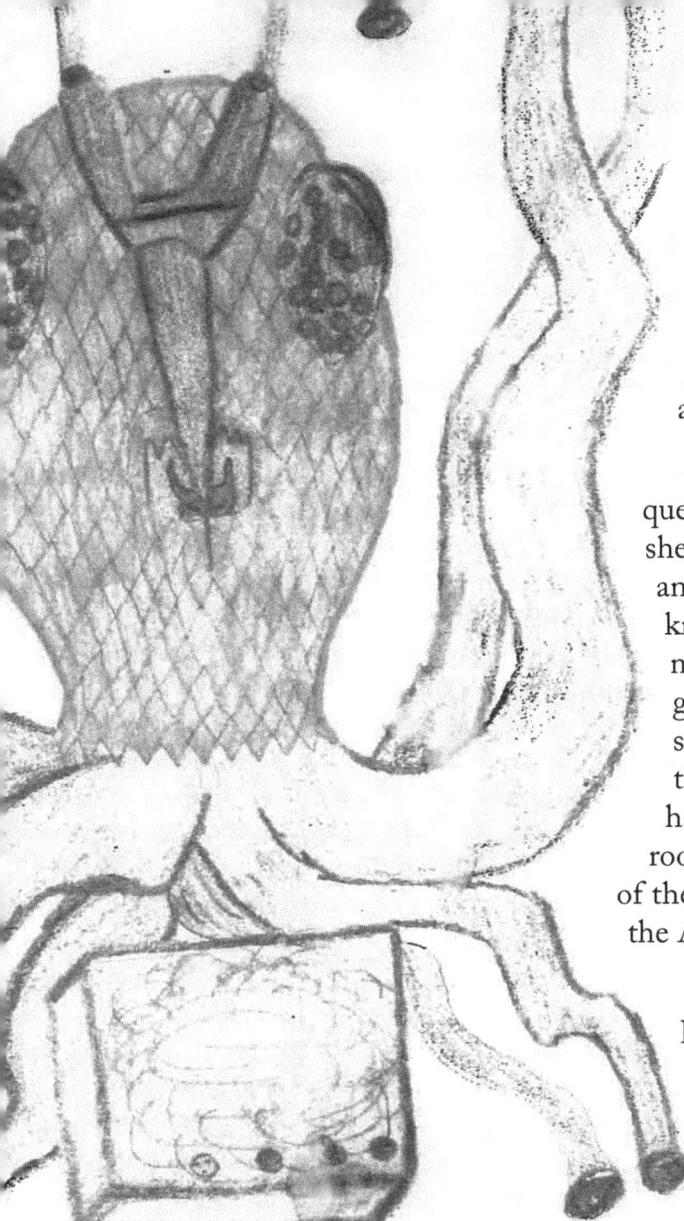

about getting herself killed so she knew that she couldn't lock herself in there with them or she would die. Now she had a way to kill them but how to trap them in the room and not get killed doing it.

She had a lot of questions in her mind but she didn't have any of the answers. She wanted to know what was these new monsters and how was she going to kill it. She now somewhat had a plan for the Aradobbles. She just had to lock them in the room and keep herself out of the room for the burning of the Aradobbles.

One day while Rosecena was fighting the monster, the doorbell rang. Belle answered the door of all people, it was Mrs. Honeybee. She wanted to visit Rosecena and her family. Belle didn't know rather to invite her in or not on the count of the monsters. So she called Tiger and asked her to go ask Rosecena about if it will be okay if Mrs. Honeybee can come in and visit for a while. Tiger asked Rosecena and she said it was okay, but let's tells Mrs. Honeybee what's going on.

So they clued her in with the horrible details and said you must be careful while you are here and then once again Rosecena was engaged in fighting, one of the monsters stabbed her with their tentacles allowing the other ones to get away. Rosecena was poisoned, she felt light headed and she tried her best to make it to the kitchen and call for Vickie. Would you get our parents please, she asked her sister? Hurry please, she urged. She was hoping that they might know a doctor with the anti-venom or someone would know what to give her to help out. She also hoped it would just wear off and she would be okay.

Her parents came and she explains that she was poisoned and that she needed the anti-venom quickly. Her heart nearly sunk when they told her that there was nothing they could do then for her that she was going to have to wait and see if it wore off and if not pray that she would get to feeling better soon.

Rosecena agreed to wait and see if she would get better. That night she woke up to a major pain in her side she then got up and started training again hoping that the distraction would help with the pain.

When it didn't work she grew really annoyed and just started searching for the monsters. She didn't know how she was going to roast the Aradobbles but she knew that she could and that she was going to have to keep her family safe. She was also hoping that it would get rid of the venom that was in her. She didn't like that she had venom in her but she was hoping that she was strong enough to handle it if not the whole kingdom was doomed.

She knew that there was thirty-nine of the Aradobbles but how would she get thirty-nine of the monsters in a room where there was a stove. Her family was out getting food; they started to head home when they saw something they thought would be nice for Rosecena. They bought Rosecena some roses as a sign of wishes for the best. They arrived home and saw Rosecena was leaning over trying to catch her breath.

The fight had taken a lot out of her and the poison was making her feel horrible. Most of all she was concerned for her family. She prayed for strength so the poison wouldn't take over. She was feeling faint but she fought through that weakness she was determined not to be the monsters victim no matter what.

She told her family she decided to use fire on the Aradobbles but there are so many of them plus she didn't know how she was going to do it. She was thinking that she was going to have to come up with an extraordinary idea to defeat them. How can we get them into the stoves? She didn't knew that there was a huge stove in the basement.

Here was her plan for the Aradobbles. She now had a great plan for them and she knew how she was going to put it into action as soon as possible. She knew that the Aradobbles love to eat animals so she asked the knights to gather up as many animals as they could instead of putting them in danger she recorded the sounds of all of the animals and put a couple recorders into the stove room that was in the basement. When the Aradobbles ran into the stove room where they heard the animals; she locked the door and slipped out, after she was out she turned on the stoves onto high.

She was hoping that they would be burned into statues. She was really happy that the Aradobbles was dead. The poison was finally gone that made her feel really happy. She was also trying to figure out what she could use on the other monster.

She wanted to tell her parents that killing the monsters had helped her get rid of the poison that was hurting her but she was worried that this other typed of monsters would hurt her. She started to search for the monsters but she didn't know where all to look she searched all of the rooms and she saw that the monsters was not in the dungeon, where would the monsters be hiding and where could she find them.

She was concern that she wouldn't find them and figure out how to kill them but she wouldn't give up hope for anything. She searched everywhere and decided that she was going to add information about the Aradobbles in her monsters book so that next time she would know. She didn't know much about the third type of monsters and had no inclination on what to do. She finally got a good look it was a strange looking monster. This monster looked like an octopus but had the head of an alligator, and it appeared to be meaner with it snarling so much at her. She asked her family to check this one out for her. She didn't know what to use on it or how to destroy it. Rosecena went looking for the monsters and found them.

She then decided that she was going to try and stabbed one but it didn't affect it in any way. She was aggravated that it wasn't working. Rosecena tried freezing them, also she tried burning them neither of those two work. She was now confused about what else to do.

She then looked down and saw that she was bleeding again and she then knew that she was poisoned again. She then heard someone ringing the doorbell, she ran to the door and there was Xena. She told her thanks for her help last time and asked what she was up too. Xena had brought Rosecena a book about the new monster and Rosecena was so glad about that.

She was grateful that she could always relay on Xena for some help. She asked Xena if she would like to come in and help her with these monsters. Rosecena knew that Xena was trying to stay out of her way so that she wouldn't get hurt but at that moment she didn't want to be alone. She knew that Xena could protect herself from the monsters and she knew that she was the best choice to have around when she had to worry about monsters.

When Xena said no thanks, I have to go and try to calm down all of the town folks. Rosecena was kind of sad that she couldn't hang out with her but she understood and said that she would see them again then. Xena then left leaving Rosecena to have to deal with the monsters and try to figure out all of the answers for any and all of the creatures she might come across. She closed the door and she started to go and check and see how everything was doing she knew that she was delaying the thought of trying to kill the monsters but she didn't want to go and fight them.

She then started to search for the creatures not knowing if she should locate their hideout or just go and read the book. She started too searched when she couldn't find anything she didn't know what to do. She knew that she was going to go and find them but where would she find them, but she couldn't track them and they were extremely dangerous. She started searching again but this time she couldn't find them either.

She decided if she couldn't find the monsters she would make them come and find her she knew that all of the monsters love blood but if she gave them blood they would get bigger and even meaner. What would she do.

She then decided not to do that and just to go and read the book. She read a lot of the book knowing that it would be fruitless to ask Xena if she knew anti-venom that might help her. Her family was in bed and she was reading the book when something attacked her all she knew about them was that they were ugly and mean she started fighting the monsters knowing that she didn't have to worry about the Kricketia anymore was a great relief to her. She was hoping that she would get to kill the monsters with some of the information from the book but she hadn't even got to read enough of the book to know how to kill them yet.

The monsters then got away and her mother came down from her bedroom she thought that she heard the door bell and she was going to see who it was. Belle saw Rosecena was still up. She asked Rosecena who was at the door. She then notice that Rosecena was still having a hard time catching her breathe. She was worried about Rosecena but she believed that she would be okay.

Belle decided that she would offer to help her daughter find out how to kill it. She then remembered what one of the knights had said and she jumped up from reading the book burn the other type she thought to herself. She sat down scanning through the rest of the book to see if it had the answer in it. She then saw that it didn't and she wrote herself a reminder about burning the Aradobbles she didn't know if it would work but she would try anyways. She knew how she was going to put the monsters to their death.

She searched the house again trying to see what she could do about the monsters and then she remembered the big stove room that you just walked into. She was worried that if she got stabbed again would she survive but she just wanted her family to survive most of all. She also didn't want any of the monsters to get out and attacked any of the people that were out in the world either. She started to search for the monsters but she didn't really want too.

She much rather knew that the monsters were all dead but she was the only way that could happened. She started to search but she found nothing again. That made her even anger she started to remember her plan and she decided that would be the best idea to do. She started to put the plan into action and that made her really happy. She told her mother she was going hunting; her mother replies by saying just hang in there. I know that you can take care of these monsters and I know that everything will work out for us somehow. To keep occupied and peace of mind Belle started cooking. Rosecena was getting back to the book in hope of something that might help her feel happier. After a while her mom came in and asked did you found anything new in the book.

She told her yes but I already knew it is a cross breed between an octopus and an alligator, it's called an Aradobbles. I know water doesn't kill them it doesn't say what does through. She was hoping that maybe Rosecena would have it figure out really soon and have it handle too. She told her that it didn't have an antidote for the poison either.

Rosecena was still reading when she heard screaming. It was her sister Rose. Rosecena ran upstairs and saw Rose injured with blood everywhere. It was a horrific experience to sees. Then the monsters came at Rosecena.

Rosecena was so mad that she grabbed a rope and wrapped the monster's tentacles together. Rosecena then decided to try cutting off its tentacles and stab it but the monsters escaped. How did it get away? She was aggravated that the monsters had got away like they did, but she wasn't going to let them get away with hurting Rose or any of the others.

She couldn't believe that she couldn't protect her sister from the monsters she was mad at her and worry that it would happen again. She knew that she needed her family with her because of the poison that was in her. She felt her full strength when she was with her family. If she wasn't with them, she knew she could handle it but at the same time she didn't want to take a chance of anything ever happening to them either.

She was concerned that she might need to send them away but she didn't want to what if she got hurt again and there was no one to help her with fighting that venom. She didn't like the idea that monsters were hurting all of the people that she cared for. She was tired of fighting the monsters and she wanted so badly for them all to be dead. Her parents came to her and asked her what she wanted to do.

She was wondering how in the world could it have got away with it legs tired up? She thought but she was also mad that she was ready to ask her family to go to Aunt Melinda but she also wanted them with her because of the poison. She was trying to keep strong but she knew that the poison was taking a lot of her strength. She decided then that she would go and ask them what they thought would be the best idea.

She didn't want to lose them so she went and asked right away. They went and vote and they then decided that Vickie, Sam, Kim, Rose, Tiger, and Troy would go and stay with Aunt Melinda because Rosecena needed her mom right now because she was a nurse. Belle went and looked at

Rosecena wounds while the rest of the family packed. Rosecena was glad that her mother was helping her but not that she would be in danger from the monster's attacking her.

Here what's Rosecena knew so far in the book. She knew that the Kricketia and the Aradobbles made these new monsters called Tickladobble. That these monsters were very poisonous and that their tentacles could still move with ropes tired around them. That's the monster had a head like an alligators with a mosquito's nose but the body was that of an octopus. It was sixty to eighty foot tall and it had scales all over it, and that fire, water, and sand wouldn't kill the Tickladobbles. Rosecena started to search for the monsters but then she remembered that she still had the Aradobbles. to take care of and now the Tickladobbles also she was starting to wish that they would quit throwing new monsters on her.

She wished that there was a way for things to go back how they used to be. When she asked her mom what to do? She was glad that she had her mother with her and she was hoping that she could make it happen. She started to wonder what was she forgetting and when she couldn't remember she just started to search again. She searched everywhere when she couldn't find the monsters she got very aggravated and decided to put her plan into action for the Aradobbles.

She started to try and search and when nothing worked to find them she started to worry that she had done something wrong with the monsters that somehow they had got away. She was pleased when she finally got a break from trying to fight the monsters.

Rosecena was trying to think what else to do about the monsters because the book didn't have any information at all about them, so she decided that she needed to get out and try to think somewhere else. She received a phone call it was the coach, he said we need all the cheerleaders at the game today. Rosecena and all the cheerleaders went to the game. They did a great job cheering on their football team. The cheerleaders had the fans having such a great time that the other team got mad at their cheerleaders. The two teams were called God sharks vs. the devils.

The devils tried everything to win but Gods sharks was one hundred to fifty points. They showed excellent sportsmanship. After the game they asked the cheerleaders and the other team if they would like to come to a party. They all went Rosecena was hoping that she would think of an idea but couldn't.

The music was loud and fun but Rosecena couldn't help not worrying about her family. Unfortunately, Rosecena's family had not done what she had asked them to do and stayed out of the house, so the monsters had scared them pretty badly that Rose was in a coma and the family was worried that they were going to lose her. When Troy called Rosecena cell phone, she got worried right away, he told her everything and she ran off to go be with her family, but by the time that Rosecena got there. Her family was praying. She walked over to her sister and said I know that that monster scared you but don't worry your older sister is going to protect you, our entire family and village from these evil creatures.

When that didn't bring her out of it she started to pray also she was so scared that she was going to lose a sister that she cried out to God. Please don't take my sister I love her and without them I am nothing but a weak little girl I know that you give me strength but so do they. I need you to leave her here with me and help me end the awful creatures that live in our palace. She finally stopped praying and looked up there was Rose staring right into her face.

Rosecena was so happy to see her sitting up that she just grabbed her and gave her a giant hug, and then the family joined in. Everyone was so overwhelmed with emotion. They were proud to have Rose back. She didn't know that the Tickladobbles and the Aradobbles had made a new type of monster. The new monster looked like a snake with an octopus body. It was called Snaketia. It had snake venom and venom from the octopus tentacles. It was even meaner than any of the others monsters.

When Rosecena returned home the second her foot touched the front door, she was attacked by all of the monsters. She turned trying to fight but there was too many. She was shocked to see snake monsters. Rosecena didn't know what to do so she fought to get to the freezer, then she threw it opened and fought to get in; she barely got the door close when the Kricketia started to freeze to death.

The Kricketia finally was all caught and in their egg but how was she going to catch the Tickladobbles, the Aradobbles and the new monster she hadn't learned much about it yet. She knew that the Aradobbles hate fire. She went to trying to kill the Aradobbles.

Rosecena started cooking dinner for her because her family was not in the house. She was wondering how she was going to burn the Aradobbles with a small stove she didn't know that there was a huge room for burning things she had forgot, but she will learn it soon or later. Finally her food got done and she went to the dining room for some wonderful dinner. She was proud to have one monster done she was hoping to have them all done soon for her family safety.

The only reason she wasn't worried about herself is because she knew that as long as she killed the monsters she would be healed. She was worried through with the Snaketia, that if she got poison that she might not survive it at all. She was really determined to keep her faith strong and steady for her family stake at least because if she gave up they might. She wouldn't even think about that through. She was hoping that Xena would show up with a wonderful book to help her again but she didn't so she was starting to worry that she might have to figure out a way to take out these monsters all by herself and that did scared her a lot.

She just wouldn't admit it to anyone though because she had to be strong not for herself but for her family and the village and all of the people in the world. She started to go and search the house to try and find the monsters but she didn't find any. Rosecena was sick and tired of the monsters attacking her and her family.

She decided it was time to kill all of these monsters but she didn't know how. She went to search around the house to see if they had a room for a pool but unfortunately they didn't, so now she knew that she would have to find another way to kill them but how. She also didn't know that none of the monsters would die by food. She knew that the Kricketia's would die by ice the Aradobbles would die by fire and the Tickladobbles would die by rose petals but the other monsters she didn't know how to kill them.

She knew that she still had to kill some of the Aradobbles and she finally had a plan to do it. She would make the monsters chased her to the boiler room then once she got them there dive out of the way and let them slide right in because she had grease the floor and it was very slick, so she put the plan in to action and got rid of all of the Aradobbles. The plan was a total success and she was very proud of how great the plan had work. Now Rosecena was trying to decide on the other monsters she knew that fire, water, rose's petals, ice, sand, wouldn't work but what could she do about the two monsters.

She went searching for the monsters and couldn't find them. Rosecena wrote down what she found out about the Aradobbles. She was glad that the Kricketia, most of the tickladobble, Aradobbles were all dead. She thought to herself at least I have two dead now if I can kill all of the other monsters I won't have any more to worry about for a while.

I might get to go to parties or anything else I want to do. She was glad to think of that. She then decided that she would get even more focused on ridding the house of monsters but she just wished that it would come on and work out. She was hoping that David would come over but he didn't then she remembers that he wouldn't be coming over anymore.

She still had to deal with the Snaketia and the other monster that she didn't know about and she didn't know how to deal with. She was trying her best to make at least a good dent in the creature that lived in the house but it wasn't going well at all and she also was concern about being injured by the creatures. She started to worry about everyone and herself being injured but she knew that she wasn't going to freak out and failed everyone that she loved.

What Rosecena didn't know was that soon she would be in an impossible battle soon because the last few Tickladobbles and the Snaketia was making a new monster that might be the end of her life. Rosecena went in to her favorite room for when she was confused. That night Rosecena woke up and couldn't get back to sleep so she decided to go exploring then she was attacked by the Tickladobbles and the other monsters. One of the monsters knocked her into a book shelf and then ran off, so she went exploring more.

She found a whole lot of aquariums it had all types of animals, sharks, fish, snakes, octopus, whales, coral, dolphins, and clown fishes. She was shocked to see all of these aquariums in the castle Rosecena wondered. Now Rosecena was determined to beat the monsters so that she could share her discovery with the family. Rosecena then decided it was time to get to testing things to kill the monsters so she told the knights to go and order a bunch of grass, and other things that might help her to destroy the monsters. When the grass didn't work she tried salt that didn't work.

She tried cactus and that didn't work. She tried some feather that didn't work. She didn't know what else to use so she started to get mad. She decided that she would try some bug poison that didn't work either but she laughed when a bunch of bugs suddenly fell from the roof. The reason she laugh is because there was no bug in the house but for some reason there was some today and they were all dying so fast.

She then started to search again when she saw that one of the monsters had got stuck it was the Snaketia. It had somehow knocked off one of the aquariums and it was stuck under it. She was going to have to put a lid or something under it so that it wouldn't escape so she grabbed the lid and trapped the Snaketia in the cage. She could now studied it and find out its weakness that alone was enough to make her feel a little bit better that she was there alone because surely if she wasn't one of her family would have got hurt and then she would be next.

Rosecena then decided it was time to get to testing things to kill the monsters so she told the knights to go and order a bunch of grass and that didn't even make the monsters show themselves so she decided to try hair that didn't work. Then she tried carpet that didn't work, she tried nails didn't work and then finally she started trying flowers she tried daisies, lilies, and then roses. When she tried roses the Tickladobbles attacked and then they ran off. It didn't waste any time at all.

After it attacked Rosecena like that she knew what the Tickladobbles weakness and she knew that it was going to be the end of the Tickladobbles. The problem was how to get a whole lot of roses to fill up the whole castle? She then decided she would ask the knights to help with that. The knight went all around asking everybody who had roses to give them it because of the monster, so everybody gave them all of the roses when they return they helped unload all the roses then Rosecena saw that they didn't have enough roses and asked them to please go and find a lot more roses.

The knights went looking and found a lady named Victoria. Victoria was a middle age lady. She had black hair. She was very beautiful no wrinkles very young looking but she had a look that she might be about forty to sixty years old.

Victoria was going to help Rosecena out but she was also a witch that was going to help her more than anyone would have guess. She was also a firm believer that God is alive and that he loves people. She was also a nurse but she mainly was a stay at home witch because she had been cursing the King and knights out for a long time. That's why the knights were nervous about going to a purple house that was a three story brick house.

They were afraid because they were told stories about the woman who lived there. One of the stories was that at night she turns into a wolf and eat anyone who comes into the woods. The second story was that she would capture and start torturing who ever she caught by her house. The third was that a giant monster lived in there and if anyone came near the house they would be ate.

That would make anyone nervous but they knew that they had to go to the house for the princess because if she fell the quest she had right now everyone in the kingdom would be sorry. They started to head to the gate to knock on the door hoping that they wouldn't die. They knocked on the door a woman named Victoria answered. They then asked if they might have all of her roses, so that they might kill the monster. Victoria asked them tell me why I should give you all my roses when you have taken my husband, my son, and my father from me?

The knight then asked how have we taken anything from you, we are not thieves. You took them to your evil king and he killed them, she cried. Oh said the knights, what can we do to make you feel better asked the knights. She snapped you can't unless you know a powerful monster killer then maybe you can but if you don't you can't help me.

We do know a powerful monster hunter her name is Rosecena athlete. She then asked them who have required you to go and get all the roses you can. The knight said Princess Rosecena you remember Prince Troy don't you how he treated everyone so nice now he has six daughters and a nice wife and they are having to worry about the monsters killing their family and the kingdom, so won't you help us all please. I want to know all his family name then I might.

What he didn't know was that Victoria was going to help in more ways than one, and what are the monsters she fighting correct names? The knights told her that she would send a Knight to go and find out the monsters name and he told Victoria, Troy family name and ages Rosecena was eighteen, Vickie was thirteen, Tiger was five, Sam was fourteen, Kim was a baby. Rose was ten, and then it's their mom Belle and father Troy.

The knight was running as fast as he could to get to Rosecena he finally arrived huffing and puffing from all the running. He was tired but he wasn't going to fell his quest and he was doing his best for Princess Rosecena. That knight had a crush on Rosecena so he was more than willing to run his self to death for her. He then asked Rosecena to write down a list of the monsters name and while she was doing that he was staring right into her eyes. Hoping that soon she would look up and he would get a better look into her face. After she had completed the list he told her thanks and he started to run to Victoria's house again.

Victoria then said I still want to know the types of monsters and who's fighting the monsters. The knight said Rosecena fighting the monsters. Just then he returned with the list of monsters. OH said Victoria I will help you, she said take all of the roses make sure you get all of them because I have five hundred roses enough to kill them for sure and I'll pray for the slayer named Rosecena.

Meanwhile Rosecena was fighting the monsters hoping to make the tickladobble step on the roses but they were to strong and fast. They had escaped as soon as they had knocked her down. She hadn't looked at her side anymore since she was stabbed because it hurt her but she looked down and saw that the bandage, wound, and venom had disappear. She was happy that the venom was gone and the wound was too but she would have been even happier if the monsters were gone too.

The knights started picking but suddenly Victoria told them to quit and all the roses was loaded into the wagons. Then she told them to take the roses to Princess Rosecena and to tell her where they got all the roses. When they delivered all the roses it filled the castled where the monsters became roses that were bright pink with black spots. That is strange thought Rosecena now how am I supposed to keep them as roses.

She was glad that the Tickladobbles were finally handled but she didn't want them to change back to monsters either. She asked the knights who gave us all of these beautiful roses? They answered by saying Victoria she was very helpful to us while we were loading the roses if it wasn't for her it would have taken us much longer to bring all of these roses. She isn't an evil witch at all she is a nice witch and I am glad that she helped us like she did.

Rosecena was starting to worry because she didn't want the roses to start wilting so she sent a knight to go and invite Victoria to join her for tea. The knights hated to drive cars so they ran to go delivered messages or they rode horses. He hoped onto a horse and took off riding to Victoria's house it was a long journey still. Rosecena was hoping that Victoria would know a secret room to lock the roses into that would keep them looking fresh and to keep the monsters locked in. That would help relax her mind and make it a little bit safer for everyone.

They arrived at the castle and Rosecena invited her to come with her into the tea room. There they sat and enjoyed tea and sandwiches for a while. You must know how to keep these monsters as roses please tell me, Rosecena asked. I will Victoria promise but I must ask something of you.

What it is, Rosecena asked. When you are done with these monsters I want you to go to my hometown in Russia and destroy only the evil, the giants, werewolves, and vampires that are there please. I will Rosecena said but only after I get it safe here. How can I keep the Tickladobbles as roses, she asked?

I know one way but you have to have a witch cursed the roses to remain in a glass dome. I wish I knew a witch that would do that for me but I don't, said Rosecena. I know a way for them to remain as roses but it's up to you if you do this then you will have to keep them under a glass dome to keep all of the monster's roses in the glass dome said Victoria. Where am I going to find a glass dome that will fit all these monster's roses.

Victoria knew about a secret room that was a giant glass dome to hold roses it was built for King Chris wife that had vanished. It could hold all of the monster's roses and all the others roses there too and make sure they stay looking fresh. Victoria showed Rosecena where the glass dome was and then they started to put the roses into the glass dome. After about two hours they got tired and hungry again.

They went and ate some more sandwiches and started talking again but it was taking so long to get that done. They were tired and now they were sweating. She was hoping that soon they would be done but no matter what they do it wasn't getting to be any less. Rosecena finally started to get annoyed and went and asked the knight if they would help them with the roses.

With all of them working together it started to go down slowly. That was a good deal but it was still taking a long time. She wanted to laugh because it was funny to her that now after all this time she was actually getting help. She was also very glad about that because she was already tired and worn out at least now she could somewhat relax now. They finally got all of the roses put up and she locked the door. Now Rosecena felt like she was getting somewhere with all of the monsters Victoria told Rosecena, thanks for promising to take care of the things that live there but then she said please keep me informed about what you find out please. Thank you said Victoria. Then Rosecena promised to keep her informed on what she found out. Victoria then left and Rosecena family came in. They asked her what's with the roses. Rosecena told them and they decided to locked the door, that led to the room. Rosecena knew that now she had to deal with the Snaketia, she didn't know about the Alligatoretia. Worst of all she didn't know how to kill the Snaketia.

She knew that she had her pets back and the family's pets so when her family came back she asked them to take the pets so that she could try to kill the Snaketia. They all left and she got ready to try and kill the Snaketia. She knew that roses, water, sand, fire and ice, wouldn't work. She had them bring a bunch of fans hoping that it would work. She was disappointed when it didn't.

She then remembered that she had one trapped so she could try a lot of stuff on it. She tried hair, nails, lilies, and roses, wood; she was starting to get mad because she couldn't seem to figure out something that might would work on the monsters. She was going to try and use coke and tea but it didn't work either. She knew that animals wouldn't work because they would eat animals.

She was confusing but she wasn't going to give up on herself and she sure wasn't going to freak out. It was nine thirty and she was ready to go and relax some because she had a headache. She went and lay down and tried her best to get rid of it. When it finally went away it made her relax some.

She finally got up and went and got herself something to eat she was hungry so she was trying to make sure that she did something good for herself. After she ate she went to the training room and trained for a while she was annoyed because she hadn't trained for a while and she had only been trying to kill the monsters. She knew that usually she would get the best ideas when she trained so she went and trained as long and as hard as she could. She trained for at least two to three hours with no stop when she started to grow thirsty she then went and got a drink quickly.

After she got her drink she decided that she would try some other things such as cactus, grass, cow dumps none of which worked. She was starting to get frustrated when her phone started to ring. She looked at the number and it was her coach. She answered it and he said that she was running late for the baseball game and they need her there quickly. She apologized and told him that she would be there soon.

The teams were the blue wings versus the Angels. The blue wings had forty nine the angels had thirty-five, so Rosecena was up to bat she hit the ball way over the fences and made a homerun which got four people home. They were all happy when Rosecena got back from rounding the bases because now they only had to get ten points and they knew that they could do it with Rosecena there.

They weren't very faithful when she wasn't there. They sent out another player and she made it to second base. Then another made it to first. Then another girl made it to base the bases was loaded and they sent out another player she got two players home, so now it was forty-one to forty-nine. There were two on base three more people before Rosecena would hit again.

Then they would need three more points unless one gets out. Then it would be more. Rosecena was watching carefully while the other three took their turn and got on the base. It was now her turn she knew that all of her team hopes was on her shoulders.

She was nervous but she knew that she could do it. She walked up to the base about to take her turn when the other team coach yelled time out. It was because one of his team mate was getting thirsty and they had run out of water. He asked them if they could show them where the water facets were.

Rosecena showed them where it was and then waited for them to come back to the field so that they could get back to the game. They were finally done and they started to head back up there. It was going to be fun playing more against this team and she was feeling so much joy that she was happy to be out playing instead of killing the monsters.

She was on the plate and hit the ball. It went past two fences and the one after that. Her team jumped up cheering when they saw that when Rosecena ran across the home plate her team was there waiting for her.

They had just passed the other team the score was forty-nine to fifty. They were so happy they did flips and cheers. Then they went and showed good sportsmanship to the blue wings they told them they really enjoyed playing them and that they should have fun on their next game too. Rosecena started to head home when one her teammates invited her to come to a party with her.

While Rosecena called her mom and asked them to stay away from the house because she had to calm herself and then she said that she will have to kill the Snaketia's and her mother said she wasn't stepping foot in there till it was gone, but I'm going to relax for a little while because I can't seem to get any ideas about killing this monsters and I don't know what to do. Okay, go but be careful please and know that we love you so much and we are proud of you. I hope that you are getting enough sleep and not missing school. I'm not missing school, Rosecena promised.

Don't worry everything will be fine she told her. Now I'll talk to you later I'm going to the party. She was about to hang up when her dad came on the phone. I love you and please don't allow anything bad too happened to you or even the village please.

We will always be careful and no matter what I will always take care of any bad creatures I can. I am very tired of all these creatures but I won't be able to sleep in till I get rid of all the creatures I can. It was starting to get late and she was getting where she didn't care so she told her parents she had to go now so that she could relax and they said okay. She went to the party and had fun at eleven she went home.

She knew that there would be another party tomorrow and she was going. She also remembers that she was going to be at the house again and she might get attacked again, and she wasn't looking forward to that. She headed to the house and the monster was waiting on her. They attacked her and then ran off.

I'm not getting enough sleep but I'm okay. I'm going to take care of the monsters and then I will get enough sleep. Rosecena, then said mom I got to go please relax I'm fine and will be okay no matter what. Now I'm going to go and relax at a party, I will be back at home by eleven the monster will die sometime soon when I find out what can kill them.

Then the house will be safe hopefully I am so sick and tired of fighting these monsters. Okay, said her mom, but don't drink any drugs. I won't Rosecena, promised. Then she hangs up and went to the party with her teammate.

She was having such a great time that at eleven she didn't want to have to go home but she had promised her mom that she would so she left. When Rosecena got home she saw the Snaketia and right away started to fight them.

She knew that she would just make it run away and knew that she was the only one in the house, there was nothing for the monsters to eat, and Rosecena made sure of that.

When the Snaketia's ran off, she tried to follow but they were too fast. They escaped before she could stop them. She now knew that she was going to have to be at full strength for these monsters because they were too fast. She went in to the kitchen made her some lunch and then after a while she got ready to try again.

The problem was where it disappeared to and why was it so fast. She then started to search again but had no luck finding the monster so she grew even frustrated and went to trying more objects on the monster that she had caught the only thing was what to use that's when she heard a loud crash it scared her so bad that she ran in there just in time to see the one Snaketia she had caught get away. She tried following but again it got away by this time she was even more aggravated because she thought that there should have been no way that the monster had got away but yet they did. The monster was so quick and Rosecena wasn't fast enough so she decided that she would go and get some tracker devices. She was hoping that she could track the monsters down then at least she would know where they are hiding and that would be a good start. She was just confused to get one that would stay on these monsters.

Two weeks passed and she was ready to try everything. She tried milk, honey, butter, woods, water, fine sand, grass, roses, and leather it didn't work so she decided to try fingernails, hair, leaves, electrified, and posters none of that Work. She went into town hoping for some ideas some idea so that she can take out the monsters she tried bread, flour then she found a lady selling beads it didn't work on the monsters. She went back into the town and keep on looking she saw a stand for dragon blood.

She didn't know rather to try that or not because she didn't want the monsters to get any bigger, but she decided that it was worth a chance.

Unfortunately, what she had hoped to avoid didn't work the Snaketia's grew even bigger so on top of being fast and mean they was even taller. Rosecena was so mad she took the dragon blood outside and hid it in the storage room. Then she went back to town and keeps looking for an answer.

The answer comes from a guy selling cotton. Rosecena asked if she could buy that from him and he told her that she could but only if she would take this beautiful golden armor, shield statues, and necklaces, earrings, bracelets, rings, and pennants. She did kind of not want to take it because what if it turned into a monster then she would have another monster to take care of.

She was also nervous of even trusting this guy because what if he knew that it could turn into a monster and it attacked her that wouldn't help her at all. She did not want to take the objects that he had offered her but she wasn't going to not give it a chance because she really wanted the monster dead. That was enough reason for her to trust this guy but she was still nervous. She was then determined that she was going to beat up the monsters now.

All of her animals were out of the house so that the monsters were all out of food except for her. Will the monsters attack her or would they just starve which she wouldn't mind either. She was tired but she was going to hunt down the monsters right now.

Rosecena asked, it don't become a monster or anything does it? No, said the man, I just thought that they would look good on you. Okay thank you, I hope that this will help me take care of the monsters problems once and for all, so then Rosecena went home with all the cotton. She was hoping that she could take it home and unload it. Then the monsters would attacked her and die. Unfortunately it didn't work that away.

Rosecena unloaded all the cotton and waited to see what would happen. The monsters growled a horrible loud growl, then it was quite again, so Rosecena now know that the Snaketia's hated cotton and she now knew she needed more cotton and a way to keep the Snaketia's on the cotton so she called Victoria, she said to Victoria you seem to know this castle really well is there a way I can trap the Snaketia's in a room with cotton. Victoria then said yes, but you must be very quick or you will be hurt. There was a steel room in the basement where you could put a lot of cotton but how to get the Snaketia's down to the basement with the cotton was the hard part because you can't let the monster's tentacles or fangs get you or you will be poisoned.

She was now worried about being poisoned because of all the tentacles and the fangs. She knew that the monsters were her main concern but still she was worried about her own life also. What if she had been poisoned by the monsters then how would she survive if that happened. She would be in the worst of danger.

She didn't have time to worry about that right now though she really must go and defect the monsters. It wasn't working through because she hadn't come up with a plan yet and she really needed to. Then she started putting all the cotton into the steel room which was a lot of hard work for one person but she knew she could do it. It was about two o'clock and Wednesday morning. She then remember that she was going to have to go and lay down for a while because if she didn't she wouldn't have any energy to fight the monsters next time they attack her. She went and lay down and she heard the monsters growling again.

She was nervous about that because she was the only one that was at the castle and she was tired.

Rosecena went and put all the cotton in the steel room, and was then trying to decide how to get the monsters into the steel room. She decided to try to lead them by animal's calls. That didn't work and she now knew that she was going to have to find a different plan because she knew that she was going to have to find a way to make the monster do what she want it to do ! Rosecena really disliked the Snaketia's because she knew that she wouldn't be able to kill it the same way she killed the kractia, so Rosecena was trying to think of ways to make it work when the alarm clock went off.

Oh no its time for school and I haven't figure out how to kill the Snaketia's yet. Their mom came down and saw Rosecena and asked "did you stay up all night again"? Yes mama I did but I am not any closer to killing the Snaketia's said Rosecena. I am glad to have three of the monsters dead, and I am glad that I almost got all the monsters dead and can't wait till I have all of the monsters dead.

Are you going to school today or do you want to go upstairs and go to sleep, Belle asked? I'm going to school then when I get back I hope I can get rid of the Snaketia. Belle was really worried about Rosecena when she insisted that she was going to school because she knew that Rosecena wasn't feeling good and that she hadn't had much sleep. She was in social studies class and she was trying her best not to fall asleep but it was almost impossible.

She jumped the bell ringing sounding the alarm for Lunch usually one of her favorite things because she knew after that came gym class which was her favorite and then they would be heading home.

Yes she thought to herself if I can make it through Lunch and even Gym I will be homeward bound. I can't wait till I can go home they had no homework and she knew that Gym wouldn't change that. She was ready to go home and kill the last few monsters if she could kill them that is. She went into the lunch room feeling ok other than sleepy from the lack of sleep she was getting thanks to always fighting monster. She loved the fact that most of the time in gym she could just lay down and sleep but today she made herself play dodge ball. Everyone thought that she was going to be out in no time but that wasn't the case at all.

They headed home, and then she started to search when Rose asked when will you be finished with these monsters, hopefully soon thank god when its done, thought Rosecena. She didn't know that the Snaketia's and the Tickladobbles had made a new monster. Her problem was how to get through school without falling asleep and how to kill the Snaketia's without more venom getting in her, because there was no anti-venom.

Plus she already knows that she had venom in her and she needed a way to make it quit burning. While she was at school that day, she suddenly got very sick she had to run to the bathroom and she threw up she lucky had one of her friend with her and asked her to go get the nurse. She then saw that the nurse came to the bathroom. Rosecena was trying to fight the throw up back.

They called her mom and told her what was happening. Her mom arrived and went into the bathroom and asked the nurse why the heck did you not take her to your office and made her lay down with a cold rag on her head. That would have helped her.

Belle helped Rosecena up then took her to the office and checked her out of school. Then she walked her to the car lay back the seat and helped her into the car. It was a little harder because she was feeling so horrible. She threw up about four to five times before she was in the car. She was really in a horrible situation because she really was that much poison.

She asked her mother where they are going. What are they going to do? She was confused and she was going to go and make some good idea. When Rosecena found out where they were heading she grew kind of sorry because she wasn't doing that great anyways and now she was going to be where someone else other than her mom was.

She really just wanted to go home and go to sleep but since that wasn't going to happen she took it as a sign that soon she was going to be healthier than ever. That made her feels a little bit happier because she knew that her mom had an idea that would help her. Then when she gets home then the monsters can disappear also. That was the best news she had all day through.

Rosecena started to apologize but her mom said don't worry about it just get to feeling better okay. I wasn't feeling bad till after gym class, I guess that I got to hot maybe. I don't know I think that it from the lack of sleep you have been getting you was getting at least nine hours asleep a day but now you are getting only three hours two times a week that's not enough, and then a lot of it could be the venom. Rosecena, I am very worried about you!

I really want these monsters gone so maybe you can get healed at least that how it worked with the last monster? I don't know but I know that one way or another I have to kill these no good for nothing Snaketia's because even if I die. I don't want you all near any monsters. Don't talk like that Rosecena, you will survive you are too tough to die by any evil creatures.

I know that God made you a tough, beautiful, popular young lady, who can take care of herself and everybody else. I am going to take you to Victoria's house maybe she can help you because I really think it's the venom. What can she do about it when we know that there isn't any anti-venom. They arrived at one-thirty Rosecena wasn't feeling well at all.

She was feeling really weak and she couldn't keep any drinks down at all. Her mother was really worried but she was keeping faith for Rosecena and her sisters because she really didn't want her daughters sick in bed for a long time. Rose was just now getting out of the hospital but she wouldn't have a bedroom to herself because they were still not living in the castle because of the monsters. Belle was praying that Victoria would have the answers because she was about to break down and cry.

She was totally stressed out but she was determined that her family was going to live happily in the castle. They finally arrived at Victoria's house Rosecena was nervous about going in because she wasn't feeling well but not because she was scared she just felt so weak and she knew that her mother was trying her best to remain strong for her even when she was scared to death. So Rosecena muscled up all the strength that she could and walked to the door. She knew that she was her family only hope and the Village if she lost to the venom then everyone might lose their lives and she really didn't like that idea.

She then knocked on the door at first no one answered but after a while Victoria answered the door. She was glad that she answered because she really didn't have enough strength to walk back to the car. Victoria then asked her to come in and have some tea and she accepted the invite. They talked for about an hour about the weather, and everything else before Rosecena decided that she had to ask her if she didn't want to die.

She then backed out because she figured that a witch could just read her mind and know what she was wanting but she didn't know that she already knew but she wouldn't answer till Rosecena came on out and ask her what she needed to asked. Then Victoria saw that Rosecena's Pride was getting in the way for her to ask her for help. She made her wait longer to find out the answer and she started to feel even worst. Finally after having to run to the bathroom fifteen times or more Rosecena grow more aggravated because she was feeling even sicker.

Let me explain what I mean please, said Belle. I did some research on Victoria and found out that she was alive way pass this decent. She was alive in the early day. When Jesus walked on the earth, and she still look like she might be thirty. I have a strong reason to believe that she might be a witch. Not just because of her looks and that information it's also because I contacted the people that built this castle they never builted that room where you have those roses and that steel room wasn't built by them either. That's strange, said Rosecena. Well if she is then I hope that she can remove the poison I have in me. I hope she can I don't know. When they arrived she talked with Victoria and before she even asked her. Victoria said sorry Rosecena, but I can't heal you but I do know how to transfer the venom to someone else there only one problem. The one who get it will die. After, Rosecena heard that she wouldn't even think about the idea. Rosecena then started to asked her if she knew a way for the venom to slow down where she would feel better, again she answer before she could get it out and again the answer was no. Now I wish I knew what to do because I have to kill Snaketia's and I'm either dying because of the venom or I'm sick because I haven't been sleeping but three hours two days of the week.

Thanks for allowing me to talk with you. Rosecena started to leave when Victoria came after her, and said Rosecena what if we transferred it into someone whom is dying already that way you aren't killing anyone, you are ending her suffering? Rosecena started to say no, when Victoria said if her heart is already giving out on her and she is surviving only by machine, you won't even then, and she don't have any family: I guess so if she is that bad off: said Rosecena. Victoria then told Rosecena that when I remove this venom you might feel dizzy, so then Victoria removed the venom, and Rosecena all at once felt like she was drowning in freezing ocean water.

After she recovers from that feeling, she stood up and said you did it, thank you so much. Then Rosecena left, mom she said she healed me. Oh that great honey, what are you planning to do about that monster through. I can't stand it one more day, I will scream; Belle said. I don't know but I want it died as much as you do. I really hate all monsters and it mainly because this is the second time.

I had been poisoned and had it removed. Rosecena was walking home, when she saw a figure approaching her from behind her. She turned around and the guy was tall, thin, handsome, but had muscles, his eyes was light blue, and he looked more like an angel then a human, and his hair was reddish brown spiky but not to spiky and he talked with a lot of manners. He was very strong looking.

She was shocked by this guy coming up behind her but she knew that she could defend herself if she had too. The guy kept coming and she started to get really nervous but she wasn't going to let him know that at all. He came closer and closer but she was determined that if anything was going too happened then she wasn't going to be the one that got hurt. She spined around and asked is there anything I can do for you. Why are you following me?

Here is what he said to Rosecena: hello my name is James Michael star and I have come to try to help you with your quest. I know that you are trying to kill all these monsters and if you will allow me too I would love to assist you please. Okay James I don't know if you can help me but if you believe that you can help me then please come on then. When they arrived at her house and Belle noticed that Rosecena was feeling better.

All at once "she said I notice that you are feeling better and who your friend is? "said Belle. Rosecena said yea and this is James he wants to help get rid of these monsters I still don't know what to do about them but as long as he want to help and don't die I will let him help me. I want to kill these monsters but I don't want anyone else to die through okay James? James asked why don't you go to the library and find out more information about the monster I have already try that, I know that the monster that I am dealing with don't like cotton at all. But I don't know how I am going to get the Snaketia's to the steel room. I have a plan said James. What is it? Rosecena said. Why don't we fill the house with cotton and then when the monsters attack or get where they can't do anything then lock them up in the steel room? I don't know if there enough cotton for that. They then put his plan into action. It was a beautiful plan: the plan was to make the monster run into the cotton room without touching either of them by slipping into the room.

They were going to put oil on the ground to make it slick and play a tape recorder in the room so that the monster would come into the room.

She was hoping that it would work but it wouldn't work. She was glad that she now had a friend to help her come up with some idea that way maybe just maybe she could see the end of all the monsters soon. Would she ever see it or would she die before it ever happened. She shake that horrible thought away I won't let that happen and with a witch on my side there no way that will ever happen. At least if I get poison she can remove it and if I get stabbed and it not that bad my mom can fix that. She was proud to have a lot of people to help her but she was really tired she had only slept a little bit and she didn't have much energy as she should. She prays to God for more energy.

They filled up the house with cotton then locked the basement door and her sister's rooms. The monsters then growled very loud and attacked. Then Rosecena threw one of the Snaketia's onto a piece of cottons. When it touches the cotton all the monsters started to flee but ran into the steel room instead of the rest of the house.

That's when they picked up the cotton and threw it on the monsters. The room had a roof where you could remove it with stairs attached to it so it made it really easy. They finally had all the cotton into the steel room, and the monsters was becoming smaller and smaller. After about an hour they became a bunch of teddy bears.

They became teddy bears. Rosecena walked into the kitchen. Her mom was in there and James followed her. They told her that they had finally got rid of the Snaketia's and then Rosecena remembered that she touched the Snaketia's and that meant she might be poisoned. She was mad when she realized that.

Oh great I've been poisoned again. Oh well she thought at least now all those monsters are dead. Rosecena then thanks James and said I don't know where you came from but I would have probably not killed those monsters for a long time if it wasn't for you. "Yea you would have," said James star, "and you might not have got poisoned if it wasn't for me I hate that you got hurt."

"Oh don't worry about it, I will be okay," said Rosecena, oh hey thanks for caring. "Yea he said and he started to leave. Hey why are you leaving? You could stay and hang out with me? She said, they started to hang out and talk with each other.

They started to talk and have a great time getting to know each other. She was very happy to have a friend to talk to because she hadn't got to talk to anyone in over three month other than at school and that was the only time. She then decided that she was going to spend as much time with her new friend as she could. They then started talking more when they heard a knock they had no idea who it was but she didn't care. It was four o'clock they sat down at the kitchen table just talking but now she was determined to go and eat and talked more.

It was now five p.m. when he decided that it was time to go home. I have to go now, because I have to go back home and check on my family. Oh okay, well thank you again if it wasn't for you anything could have gone wrong. Thanks to you nothing did.

Then he left and Rosecena went and unlocked the doors she locked because of the Snaketia's. Then she called Victoria will you transfer it again to a person who is dying please. Yea but be careful please because I still need you to kill all the creatures that are there but I have a feeling that it's still got monster's in it. Oh okay, well I will but I need the poison out please.

Victoria then removed the venom and Rosecena joined Victoria for tea again. After their tea, Rosecena went home. It was seven o'clock pm and Rosecena was helping their mom with diner. After the family washed all the dishes, the family sat down and played board games and hang out together. They all were all so happy because they thought that all the monsters were dead.

The next morning was Wednesday, it was Christmas day. They woke up so early and ran to wake up their parents. "Can we open the presents now please"? They asked. Not till you all go away and let us come downstairs their parents said.

The girls didn't know what to do so they went and got changed into their favorite clothes. They were very happy that soon they would be opening presents and soon they would be able to spend the day with their parents and their sister's that made them even happier. After they finished changing from their night clothes into their wonderful clothes. They planned to spend as much time as they could together.

They were patiently waiting because they knew that Rosecena was going to want to spend as much time with all of the family as she can. They were finally monster free so they thought. She knew there was another type but while the monster wasn't attacking anyone she was going to rest up and spends time with her family. She was happy for the first time in a while because no matter what she was away from monsters and was getting to relax. How long was it going to last she didn't know but she was going to keep trying to relax.

They then went downstairs to wait on their parents being very patient but they wanted the gifts right then and there, so they pace back and forward and waited. When their parents finally came downstairs they found the girls in the living room waiting on them. The girls then said, now can we? Then the girls ran and jumped closed to the presents.

They were so excited, that their parents then gave them each one gift to open each. After, they had opened the first presents the girls was even more excited because they had got one of the item they wanted. Rosecena had got a new laptop. Vickie got a printer; Tiger had got a new TV.

Sam got a trained white tiger. Rose a pair of new shoes, Kim got a baby bottle. Then they opened the others gifts. A week later they got back to having fun instead of having to worry about their sisters fighting monsters and getting hurt. They were playing x-box, their computers and everything else they wanted to do.

They were happy that they could have everybody they loved back home and that they was all not injured. The girls went to play outside when they was told they needed to go clean their rooms and take care of their pets. They went to clean their room and then started to take care of their pets. After they finished that they went and ate breakfast.

Then they went outside and jumped on their bikes. They saw deer's and rabbits and all kind of animals while they were riding and they were having so much fun. They then got stopped by one of the village person and asked to help her. They stopped and helped him. It wasn't that hard to do but for him it was because he was short and he wasn't very strong at all. The girls started to do the work he gave them to do. When they were done they started to head home. The girls were having so much fun that they didn't even bothers to worry about how far they were going. They then was stopped by another person and asked for helped the job was really easy but it took a little bit of time to do. They all were glad when they were finished with this task too. They traveled a little bit farther when they saw that it was getting dark they decided that it was time to head home.

They rode for two hours, then rode home and went to take a bath. After their baths they decided to go and see a movie they all decided to go watch Cats. They enjoyed the movie and then went shopping. They bought three dresses each.

Then went to twilight their favorite shopping and eating place. They was so thrilled that they was getting to have fun because they wasn't having all that much fun when Rosecena was having to fight all those monsters. Now that the monsters were gone they could have all the fun they wanted to without having to worry about any monsters. Then they came home and they were really tired.

That night they all slept perfectly. The next morning they all ate breakfast then the girls went too trained. They did a great job and then took a shower and they got dressed. Then they went and talked to their parents.

They wanted to do something but they didn't know what to do? They decided to walk through a zoo. They saw all types of animals and enjoyed it. Then they went to the movies and watched a movie called Rose's World. The movie wasn't that great but they didn't care because they were all together at least.

They hated the movie so much. They loved their parents more than anything in the world. They all went back to the zoo after they didn't enjoy that movie and they saw all typed of animals such as monkey's, snakes, zebra's, lions, alligators, bears, wolves, tigers, skunks, deer's, and all other creatures. The other places they went were the amusement park. They got to ride all the rides and they really enjoyed it.

After that they decided to go and ride more rides. They were growing more entertained by the minute because they were finding more and more wonderful things to do while they could because she was going to have to fight more soon or a later. She knew that and she wasn't going to allow it to take over her life and give her no entertainment at all. She was determined that some good things was going to happen to her and she was going to make sure that happened.

She was now hungry alone with her sisters she went and found their parents. They told them that they were hungry and they would like something to eat please. They then went to Charlie Chinese restaurant. They enjoyed the whole day. When they got home they went right to bed and slept all through all the night.

The next morning, they woke up then ran downstairs. There they saw their grandma, but they didn't know that she was their grandma. No offence but do we know you? Rosecena asked. No but your father does, said the lady.

Go get our father please because I want to know who this stranger is, ordered Rosecena. Tiger went and got their dad and he didn't know her. I'm sorry, but who you are, Troy asked. Troy you don't recognized your own mother? The lady asked.

No, dad told me that he killed my mother, said Troy. He didn't because one of the knights helped me escaped but barely you see he did try, he sent knights into our room to kill me but Mr. Paul Shark warned me and a good knight helped me flee for my life I had to let him and the good knight worry about you because if I didn't there would be no one that could help Rosecena kill those monsters. I'm sorry I am just now showing up you see when I did escaped I stepped on a bomb and had my whole leg blown off. I hope that you don't hate me for leaving you with that horrible, cruel, heartless, figure of a man that beat people for silly thing.

I don't hate you I just wish that I know that you were alive that way I could have found you. I love you and I wish that I wouldn't have believed what that horrible guy had said. I am thankful that they protect you and that they protected me when it came time. They really saved our family and I am pleased that they did that for us.

I can't believe that we were so protected that both me and my mother survived and thanks to them I am Paleontogist and one of the best. I am very thankful for everything the knights done for me. I am also excited that I am allowed to see you now even after my daughter has taken care of the monsters. What I didn't know was how tough she is, so strong and she loves to be strong.

She fight creatures really well while still having some kind of weakness in her like poison. He was worried because he didn't want anyone hurt.

I believed the horrible things he said and how he described your murdered was very terrible. I had trouble sleeping for a long time after that. I am so glad that when it came time for him to die they took me away to Louisiana. I would have never dream of falling in love so deeply with Belle, asking her to be my wife and then having six beautiful, independent daughter's with so much strength and love for each other that they can beat up a whole lot of monsters and keep each other alive.

I'm very proud of my daughter's and you will be proud of them too. You just have to trust that they can do it. These girls are so well behave that I can count on them to not let anything get broke and that item will be okay. You are very fortunate to have such great kids said his mom.

You are also very lucky to have a great attitude about life, and a great wife. I was wondering can I spend time with the remaining family, I have or do you wish for me to leave, said their grandma. You can stay here and live with us forever, said Troy. Just one thing if Rosecena says to get out of the house then get out because that means there is a sign of danger. Rosecena was happy that she was getting to know her grandmother and that her mom and dad were very happy.

The girls were all happy because now their father was at least with his mother. The girls wanted to go riding to give their dad and grandma a chance to catch up with each other. They asked if they could go and ride their bikes so that their grandma and dad could catch up with each other but right away they were told no because they needed to spend time with their grandma. They went and sat down beside their dad and waited for them all to start and talk again.

Then grandma asked Rosecena how bad the monsters were, did she enjoyed fighting the monsters or did the monsters hurt her at all Rosecena answered and told her that the monsters did hurt her and that she hated the monsters because of the poison they have. All of their pets were finally being brought in to the castle and they all were really happy about that. Now that they had everything and everyone back together they were ready to cheer up a storm.

Rosecena was happy to see her father happy, but she hoped for their sake that all the monsters were dead. If not then she hoped that she could defended them from the monsters. Where am I going to sleep Troy, asked

Grandma. He found the perfect room for her and then unpacked. Dad I am worried, said Rosecena.

What about Rosecena? Troy asked. What if I didn't kill them all? What if they have been mating this whole time and made a whole lot of the Kricketia's, the tickladobble, the Snaketia's, and any other monsters they might make? Then what the castle got a lot of people in it now and if they attacked the people will not be patient to get out of here?

What are we going to do then? I can barely hold off the monsters, I don't know how I'm going to beat them if they all attack at once. I also have to make sure I don't touch the Snaketia's because they will poison me. Don't worry sweetie we will think about this in a little while in your room.

He stayed and hangs out with his mother a little while longer while Rosecena went down stairs and started to try and find out more about all the monsters. They were all happy because they were all together again. The girls were all ready for some good news and they knew that all the girls were talking again for hours. The girls went riding on their horses and bikes they had a lot of fun and then they went and trained again.

They trained long and hard but they were having so much fun they didn't see their grandma and dad come to watch them trained. When they saw that they jumped down and went to see what was up. Their dad came and told them that their grandma came to see them trained. The girls went back to training they trained long and hard and they didn't mind it because they knew that they could do it without hurting themselves.

The girls then got tired of training and wanted to go and take their break so that maybe they could regain their energy. They went and took their bath and then went and relax so that when the girls was tired they were happy about being able to relax and knowing that their sister was safe from the monsters. That's was a blessing and they didn't know that it was also a curse. They didn't knew that at this moment none of the girls was actually safe.

Rosecena and her parents was in her room. We don't want any panic; we just want to be prepared, said Troy. Yea, dad you are right I don't want a panic, but I want to know that everyone is safe forever. Later that day, the girl's grandma called to them. Hey girls, the reason I called you was becomes I want to spend some time with you all if you don't mind.

At first they thought that they weren't going to have any fun, but they found out different. She took them to a rollercoaster park, where they had a blast. They rode every ride in the park. Then they went and ate.

Then they went to the moon shuttle and got to float around, and bounce around. By the time they were heading home the girls were so hungry, that they begging their grandma for something to eat. She gave in and they ate at Ryan's they enjoyed all the good food. Then they continued heading for their home. The girls were fast asleep.

Then grandma stopped the car and got some of the knights to come and help her get her grandchildren into the house. They did and the girl's parents grew worried, "what happened to them?" they asked. They had too much fun today so they fell asleep. They put the girls in their bed and then exit the room.

The parents was happy that their girls was so incredible happy. While the girls were having a good time they were also concerned about any more problems. They didn't want to think about that because that made them worried because they could lose their sister. Who knew what else would happen but they prayed nothing bad would happened.

They only want the best for them and the village where they live for now and ever hopefully. The girls was also glad that because the monsters was gone for now and hopefully forever. She was determined that somehow all the monsters everywhere would be died. She was determined and happy.

They know that everything was going to be okay but they hope and pray that their daughter would never have to fight anymore monsters again. They really hated all monsters and wanted to ensure that everyone was safe. The girls then woke up and saw that somehow they got in their bedroom and was shocked, because in their room there was a massed wave of presents. Who could these be from?

They got up and started to open all of them. The gifts were from their grandma. They loved every last bit of the gift. It was everything that they wanted.

They ran to their grandma and gave her a huge hug. That made her so happy that she gave them a bigger hug. Then the girl's parents came checking on them and got pulled into a hug too. Then Rosecena was told to look outside in the front yard. This gift wouldn't fit in your room, so I hope it what you wanted.

Rosecena ran to the door and saw a beautiful pink ford mustang on the hood of the car it had roses to the back of the car then it had puppies on the doors. She was so happy she let out a scream before she could stop herself and ran to her grandma and said thank you it's the exact car I wanted and its perfect. I love you, my sisters, and my parents I can't believe how lucky we are to have such a great family. She was impatiently waiting on dinner to be done but it was taking a long time.

The girls were all so happy that they were able to be with their family and now she was eating they was still too excited for everything. They knew that was going to be able to go and ride in Rosecena's new car, now they was wanting to go to the movies with Rosecena's new car and ride with all their families to the movies. However that wasn't going too happened because they knew that their dad was going to make them eat dinner before they could even think about going to the movies. The girls were so excited they wanted Rosecena to drive her new car for a while.

Can I drive it now, Rosecena asked; "Not yet, you have to come and eat first," said their dad. Okay, I'll eat then I get to drive my new car right. Yes, but you might want to see all the other presents first, he said. "What other presents?" the girls asked.

Your grandma has bought you all a bunch of presents and she wants to see the looks on you all faces when you all open the presents. They ate breakfast and started to open the gifts, they loved all the present. They each had five hundred presents each. The other girls started to play with their new wonderful items.

Rosecena got in her car and drove around with her dad. They had a fantastic time and Rosecena was really proud that she got to drive her new car. When they got back home Rosecena was even happier. Then she went and pet on her new horses.

Rosecena loved horses, she wanted one since one saved her from a pack of wolves while she was chasing some monsters in Italy. She would have been bit by the wolves but the horse jumped right in the way and bunked the wolf that was about to pounce on her. Rosecena walked into the house and gave their grandma a huge hug and then said thanks you for all these gifts they are wonderful. I just wished that I would have got you something.

That's okay sweetie just seeing all of you so happy is what I wanted. It's the best gift that I could ever get from you all. I love you girls, and your parents. You guys have a good life to live now that those monsters are going down. Then Rosecena got to thinking what if all the monsters are not dead what if they were just hiding gaining strength like Victoria had said.

Then they might all have problems and what if she gets poison again. She might die and not be able to save herself. She knew that her family would survive because she would make sure that they are out in time but what about herself she couldn't be sure that the same would be successful for her. She knew that if she could remain strong enough then she could do it but if not then she was in trouble.

At least now, I know that you all cannot be killed by those awful monsters that used to live here. "You are a real hero Rosecena, you know that right? If it wasn't for you killing the monsters we would all have to be worried since we was afraid that the monsters would one day kill everyone, said Grandma. Yea, thank God I can kill all types of monsters, Rosecena said. I hope that I haven't said anything to upset you, said Grandma.

No it's just that everyone but I knew about the monsters and they almost ate my sisters but somehow I kept that from happening," Rosecena said. Plus I am worry that the monsters might accidently get out again because some are frozen in an egg in the freezer and the maid could get them out then I have to worry that everyone get out safely if that happens. I think that I'm going to get mom to put a freezer in my room so that I don't have to worry about those monsters. You are right sweetie someone should have told you about those monsters it wasn't fair that you have everything on your mind right now.

We are going to get you a freezer in your room for those eggs. Then you can worry about school only wouldn't that be nice? Grandma asked. Yea that would be nice, but that won't be the only thing I have to worry about, said Rosecena. When we get back to the house we will start and work on that freezer for you okay? Grandma asked.

Are you sure a freezer won't be too expensive. That doesn't matter to me as long as you know that the monsters won't be able to get away then that all that matter right said Grandma. Yeah that true and I'm very proud to be able to have you in my life at less I now know I can lock the eggs up and not have to worry about them thanks grandma. I'm very glad that somehow everyone will remain safe and no matter what the monsters will remain eggs.

She was also thinking what to do about Victoria's problems. She at least knew that the problems were getting to be less because she took out a few of the monsters and she had to work on the rest of the monsters now. She was going to kill every monster one way or the others she thought in her mind at least. She knew her will power was that strong?

I am always busy and I love it but I don't like when my family or friends are in danger. I am going to be going to take care of more monsters soon, but I hope that it won't be where my family can get hurt. Well don't worry things will get better. You are so capable of defecting every monster in the world; I have that much faith in you.

Plus I bet that you are able to win against giants or anything else like that. You are just that wonderful; you are an incredible young woman. I know that you can do everything to kill those evil monsters, and they won't hurt you. You are a slayer; you got special powers to make it where nothing can hurt you.

Thanks grandma, that really make me feel better, said Rosecena she walked into the house and saw her family all talking. Hey what's up? Rosecena asked.

Belle ran up to Rosecena and gave her the biggest hug. Your sisters out of the coma she can come back home.

Rose is alright, do you think we all should go pick her up, or let your dad? I say let's all go say hey to Rose. It will do us all some good. Then they all left the house to go see Rose, when they got there they was all so overwhelmed with emotions that they all gave her continuous hugs. Then they all left the hospital and started on their way home, but the girls wanted some ice cream, so they stopped and got some.

After they all enjoyed their ice cream they continued to head home. Before they even thought about going home they went to the circus and got to see all types of animals they was so happy to see that they were gone for hours. After they enjoyed themselves at the circus they started to head home again three of the girls was riding with Rosecena and the others with their dad. They were so happy that they could relax and get to see some enjoyments with their families that made their days a lot better.

They started to head back home when they receive a call. It was grandma calling Troy. She wanted him to keep them out longer. She wouldn't explain why through but he agreed to do what he was asked.

They all were so ready to go inside but their dad wouldn't allow that. They went to eat Crawfish and Shrimp before they would go to their house. When they arrived home they didn't notice any of the boxes that were in the front yard. They got inside, then grandma yelled stop!

Rosecena was shocked by that so she asked her what was going on? You remember how you told me your worries; well I fixed it for you. Come and see. Now you have a place for those eggs where you won't have to worry about any mishaps happening.

Rosecena went and seen what was making her grandma so excited. When she saw it, she gave her grandma a great big hug, now there's no way that the eggs will hatch again. I also won't have to worry about the Aradobbles because they burned up. The other's I have locked up with iron locks, and at least I know that they are safe because I'm the only one with the keys to those locks.

I know that all the trouble of those awful monsters will be dead soon. Can her troubles really be over? Then Rosecena ran to her family and told them that the eggs wasn't going to drive her crazy anymore and her family will be safe for now on. I am so glad that all the monsters are either dead or locked up tightly.

They all went to bed after she hugged her family again. That night they all woke to the sound of knocking on the door. They were shocked to hear all of that, Belle went to discovered who it was and saw a very strange lady. The lady was very old had long black hair and she was searching for Victoria.

She was tall and very thin. She had long nails and she was kind of creepy looking. She didn't know what to think about this lady but she knew that Rosecena wouldn't be afraid of her. She was really scared of this lady but she wasn't going to let her know it.

She was kind a nervous so she called Rosecena to get her to come downstairs because a lady needed some help. She was glad when Rosecena finally came down the stairs because she didn't want to be by herself with this woman.

She was confused when she saw the lady standing in the door way she was thinking to herself does this lady have any idea what time it is?

She was downstairs and her mother told her that this lady is looking for Victoria. Rosecena then asked what you want me to do through. Rosecena asked. Would you please take her to Victoria's house please? Rosecena then got some clothes on and went and started the car they headed to Victoria's house.

They got to Victoria's house and Rosecena went and woke Victoria. Then she explained about why she was there at this kind of time. It was four o'clock am and she was going to help them and go home to go back to go to bed, but they had a different planned. Rosecena started to leave but then they shouted hey Rosecena wait, we still need you.

What do you mean by that, Rosecena asked. Why do you two need me at four in the morning? What am I supposed to do and can it wait till maybe six, seven or later? Rosecena relax, said Victoria. All we need you to do is to beat those monsters.

They are all dead, said Rosecena. No they are not before you got rid of the Snaketia's they and the tickladobble had made babies and those new monsters are very mean. These new monsters are even more poisonous and worst temper than any you ever fought before. Just be ready, these new monsters are more aggressive than ever before.

Then why haven't those monsters attacked us yet. Do I always have to hunt every monster down? Can't they ever just all die? Don't worry these monsters will die out soon enough. That really upset her but she wasn't going to take out her anger on them if she could help it.

She was about to leave but she decided that she should stay and wait because she didn't want to keep being wake up. She expected that Victoria wasn't ready for her to leave yet. She was waiting for one of them to come over to her and asked her whatever it was that way she could go get in her car and go and sleep. She expected that something was still wrong but she didn't know what else to do she didn't want to take forever to get everything done and she was ready for bed.

She was going to make sure everything was ok before leaving because she was going to turn off her cell phone when she got home. That would ensure that she get some sleep. Now what do I do then? Rosecena asked you go home and looked for them find them and try to kill them but know that what you used before will not work with these, you have to use something new but I don't know what that is. Sorry I wish that I could help. They then went to talk to Victoria, then came back to Rosecena and said you will need to be careful because their venom is more deadly than the others.

Okay now what, she snapped. Go home and rest in the morning or when you feel better than you can start to searching and killing those awful monsters. Rosecena then went home and fell right asleep, she was ecstatic to finally be asleep. She was still asleep when the alarm went off to wake her for school.

She got so aggravated that she hit the alarm with all her strength, and broke the alarm clock. That day at school, they all had a good day. They were really excited especially when they got home. They got home and started on their homework and training.

They started tending to their wonderful pets. The reason they was so excited was because their parents had promised to take them to an amusement park. They would be able to have all the enjoyment they wanted too. When Rosecena recalled what Victoria had said right then she got really mad and said that she wouldn't be able to go with them because of more creatures. She was frustrated but she had to do what she had to do so she told her family that she couldn't go with them to the amusement park she had to go and fight more monsters. Her parents was very confused by that because they believed just like she had that she had the monsters was all dead.

They also knew that she was tired so they thought that she was just making up things so she could go back to bed. When she insisted that she had to kill the other monsters they knew that she wasn't lying. They agreed with her and said go and kill the monster and make sure that you kill them all. I am going to try my best at killing them all but it might take a while because I have no idea where they might be. She was happy that her family understood what she was saying.

Belle said I understand and will be praying for you. I wish that they were all dead but Unfortually not this one is extremely dangerous. I don't know what its weakness is so fighting this monster is going to be even harder than any other monster is going to be ever harder than any other monster. I have ever fought ever before. "You do know that you can wait a week or two then try to take that last monster out right you don't have to rush into fighting them? Why don't you wait and then when it attacks you then try to take it out?" asked Belle. Mom if I wait then how am I going to find out what its weakness is and where its hideout is? I know it's in the castle but will it hide in the basement or somewhere else? Or does it keep moving? Plus what do I need to avoid? I know only about its poisoned where is the poison at I need to know ? I know that Victoria can transfer it but what if I can't get to her in time? What if it's too powerful for me? She was worried but then she started to pray that she wouldn't have to worry about any of that? "What do you want us to do?

Belle asked. "Stay home or go to the amusement park? "Go on to the park just because I can't go doesn't mean that my sister have to suffer. "Rosecena said. She was going to destroy all the monsters and make everything work out. She decided that she would go and search for the creatures again. She went and search for her animals and then she decided to search for the monsters again. It was difficult to make the monsters come out so she can destroy all the monsters.

She was growing very impatient however she didn't want to have to fight a huge amount immediately. She was searching but wasn't succeeding it aggravated her but she dealing with it. She decided it was time that the monsters die because she was fed up with them always being in the way. She wanted to continued searching but she was tired and decided to go get some food. She figured it would give her strength and help her plan better, her mom comes to her while she is eating.

Your very brave Rosecena I wouldn't have even tried to kill these awful monsters, Belle complimented. Thanks Mom Rosecena said. When these monsters are gone then it will be great no more dangers at this kingdom. Then I can kill those creatures for Victoria and then maybe relax! Rosecena exclaimed. I would have loved to come but might as well go on and get rid of the evil before it try to kill everyone. I just hope it work out for me because if it take forever to kill this one then I am going to get very annoyed.

Everyone should probably leave through because I won't be able to defend everyone while fighting these monsters. I will be okay because I can take care of myself. I just hope that I can defect them quickly without being poisoned because I don't plan on dying and I don't know if I will be able to fight this venom. Her family then left alone with everyone else.

Then Rosecena went to her room and grab her flashlight and body armor just in case of poisons. She hoped that it would defend her from being poisoned. She then started to search again for the monsters but she didn't know anything about them but she knew that it was time for them to die. She started in her room and didn't find them.

She started searching for the monsters everywhere. She was tired and was determined that something was going to work. She knew that it might take a while but she was determined that it was going to work out she just didn't know how. She was pushing herself harder because she was determined to make it work out no matter what.

She knew that she needed to do more stuff but she didn't know what to do about that yet. She needed to go and work on her room and she needed to do something about her training. She had been training but not as much as she would like to do. She also wasn't running around with her pets and not getting to do anything she wanted to other then to kill all of the monsters that the only thing that she has done this whole three months she has been trying to take care of some of her problems.

She searched her sister's room and parents. Then she searched the kitchen. After that both bathrooms. Then suddenly she heard the doorbell ringing, she thought who could that be and headed that way to see who it was? It was James Star. "Hey" Rosecena said. James said" hey," Rosecena said. I want to help you if you don't mind, James offered. Okay but you have to be careful not to get hurt. I am going to get very mad" Rosecena told him.

Then they both started to search for the monsters. They searched the dining room and the knight's room. Then they searched the maid's room still nothing. They was about to searched the attic, when the doorbell started ringing again .It was Emily; she had come to find her brother and take him home.

Emily was very pale skinned, blue eyes. Her hair was long and wavy bright with orange highlights. She had long nails painted pink with white spots.

She told James that Ralph sent her to find him because he needed to come on home. He left with Emily they left so fast that she wished that they could get to know each other before they had left. She was going to start searching again when she heard a loud knock. That alarmed her so she went to start searching again she heard the loud knocking continued.

She went down again and she saw James had returned that shocked her again hey how are you. I've came to help you and I mean it. Oh okay well I'm happy that you are here. At least now I have a better chance to get rid of the monsters now and thank God for you.

She was so happy that she didn't care about much other than making the monsters disappear and getting to visit with James that what she wanted but she didn't know how long that was going to work. She then knew that it was going to work out because she had some help now. They heard another loud knocked and James said Oh dang it what is she doing here. She was surprised when he said that because she didn't know who it was and they then went and saw that it was Emily again.

Then James left with Emily leaving Rosecena to locate, the monster and destroy them if she could ever find them. She then went into the attic and found them. She got a good look at them. It had a dolphin body of an octopus the legs had alligator head all over them.

It had eight legs. It was brown with snake head all over its back and then sharp thorn poking everywhere else venom all over every thorn and teeth. It had wings like a butterfly, and it was only three feet tall. She noticed it was hissing at her and striking at her too.

She jumped back right in time to keep from getting hit by one of its fang. Then she turned back around and saw that the monster's had vanished. That made her pretty mad because she thought that she would be able to to have it dealt with or at least wounded. She went back down stairs to calm herself down but it wasn't working.

Then the phone rang. It was James he was calling to make sure she was okay. She stayed on the phone with him for at least two more hours. When James said that he was coming back over to help with the monster she almost jumped in happiness she really liked him. She then asked him what time was he coming over so that she could let him in without the monsters getting out?

He told her that he would be over there really soon after he said that the doorbell rang and she ran to answer it, she saw that it was him and she almost jump in his arms from all the happiness in her heart at that moment. She knew with him there would be no way she died because the monsters was about to die and soon she was going to get to relax and there would be happiness again. James had the same thought in his mind but he wasn't going to let her know that because he didn't know if she had the same idea or not. He could see that she was happy but that's all he could see.

Rosecena then asked what you want to do. Hug or hunt the monster in her mind she was thinking hugs him but she knew what she needed to do. She was okay. They talked for about two hours, when he asked about the monsters. She didn't want to hunt them, she wanted to hug him.

She told him all about the monsters. Then he asked if she was okay, to him she sounded depressed." I am because I almost had the monster at least stabbed once but instead, I jumped out of the way before it hit me." She said. James then said" please don't be upset about that, I don't want you hurt either."

I just wish that I knew a way to kill these monster's I want these creatures out of my family house, so badly it is such a pain to fight these monster. "Sorry about having to leave you like I had to," James apologized. It's okay maybe next time we can sit down and drink tea or something," Rosecena said." Who know, maybe I just want to see you," James said.

"Oh okay, you have an amazing way to tell someone you like them and thank you. I really want to see you too, and I hope it soon. You are a really nice guy and I want to get to know you. I want to ask you something but I want to ask you in person, okay when would you like to ask me because I would like to make sure that the monsters don't interrupt us when you come over again.

I don't know because I don't want to put any of you in any danger at all.

Okay come over whenever you want to till then know that the monsters are going to die soon or a later. The monsters then growled and she knew that they didn't like what she had said but she didn't care at all. She wanted to kill them now but she was worried because without the star clan being there she knew that she was in a lot of danger still. She wanted to be able to read books and go and try to do what she had to do about all the monsters go out with her boyfriend and then maybe go and kill the creatures in Russia.

That what she wanted to do but she didn't know how that was going to work out either. She was believing for the best but she still knew it was hard. James and Rosecena hung up and she went to search for the monsters, she was hoping to find them. She was hoping that the monsters would come and hunt her down but it didn't work at all.

Okay, Rosecena said. Then they both hung up and James talked to Ralph because he wanted to ask Rosecena to be his girlfriend. Ralph told him it would be okay but you will have to be honest with her. I mean about you being a vampire too. James agreed but he was nervous about telling Rosecena that he was a vampire.

He went and bought her a beautiful ring and then traveled to where Rosecena lived. He was going to give her the ring as a sign of them being in a relationship. She was in the attic looking for those monsters when the doorbell rang. She was shocked, but she went to checked and saw Xena she had brought her another book.

Xena then said I hope this will help you out some. I don't know if it will but just maybe it will. Then Rosecena grabbed it and started to look for this new monster and found nothing about this new monster. She told Xena thanks anyways because she was trying to help even through it was really dangerous.

Rosecena knew that ice, fire, cotton, grass, and roses petals wouldn't work.

She then remembered about the secret room and thought maybe that can help me. She started searching for the monsters because she knew that one way or the other something was going to work out and she hoped for the best even if she was scared. She started to search everywhere but she could see that she wasn't having any luck at all.

She knew that the monsters all had different weakness. She was hoping for the weakness of the Snaketia and the Alligatoretia's but none of it was working. She then decided to go and start searching again and the monsters growled.

She started to get annoyed but nothing was working again. She worked on another problem then she saw that she wasn't doing any good so she went and got some food in her stomach. She ate her favorite food some tacos. She also had some sprite for her drink and she went and watched TV while she couldn't think of a way to find the monsters or kill them. After relaxing for a little while she decided that she needed to go and hunt the monsters again so she started to search again.

Then she heard the doorbell ring again. She ran over to it and there was James. He said Hey beautiful, how are you? How about we kill these monsters and then we talk for a while? Where haven't you looked yet?

I haven't looked in the basement but why don't we talked first. She wanted to spend time with him before hunting the monsters. We will be able to spend a lot of time together believe me on that James assured her. Then they went into the dining room and saw Xena, before James could ask she introduced Xena to James.

Xena then decided that she needed to leave so that they could find the monsters, but before they had the chance to start looking they heard the doorbell it was Ralph. She was about to asked him, may she help him when James spoke up and said Rosecena this is my dad he wants to come in just in case, we get hurt he is a doctor. They agreed that would be okay and then all three of them started to search for the monsters and they was very annoyed when they didn't find them in the basement. Well where do we search now, or do we start searching everywhere again? Rosecena asked

She was kind of worried about leaving Ralph in the castle when they were going to be searching for the monsters. James could see that something was bothering Rosecena so he said not to worry because he could take care of himself and he is just worried that one of us is going to get hurt that's why he is here. She was concern for his safety so she reliantly agreed to let him stay in the castle with the monsters running around. They started to search for the monsters when something gave her the bad feeling like something was going to happen that she needed to worry about.

They all three started searching with three of them looking it went a little bit faster then she expected. That pleased her but she couldn't believe that they didn't once see the monsters. They started to search again but it was no good they didn't find the monsters again. That really annoyed her because she knew that the monsters didn't get out and that they should have found the monster's by now.

They decided to split up and search everywhere again, but as they were about to start they heard the doorbell ringing. When they got there it was all of Ralph family. They asked, if they could help too? They then started to come in when Rosecena started to object to that but James assured her that they would all be okay.

She was mainly worried that one of them would be hurt. Rosecena, I want to tell you something right now okay? We are good vampires, we don't drink human blood only deer or bad vampires venom. You are vampires; well at least you are the good type not the evil. I can handle that, I knew that there was good vampires but where, I didn't know that part. I refused to kill the good vampires because they have helped me out a whole lot.

Without good vampires one time, I would have been killed all ready. Ralph then decided to asked what she meant by that. She then started to explained, I went to Russia when I was fourteen because people kept telling me that they was being attacked by giant wolves. I checked it out and was having a hard time destroying these werewolves but then a bad vampire attacked me and I had to fight not one thing at a time but four werewolves and two bad vampires all at once.

When I thought that I was about to die a tall figure walked out of the shadows and attacked a werewolf and then three more vampires appeared and started helping me. Thank God, that those vampires showed up because I was sure that I wasn't going to survive without their help. Then Ralph asked, Rosecena do you think that you can describe them?

She said tall, that's all I can remember because it was dark and I was still fighting some werewolves. I also remember that one of them had brown hair and brown eyes because one had to suck the venom out of me. He was tall and handsome. Well I need to kill these monsters but I don't know how to do that yet. You know anything about these types of monsters its first types is Kricticia, the first three types are dead. These new type is really quick and I hope that we can kill them quickly.

Thanks you guys for everything. I am glad for the chance to work with you guys on killing these monsters. I am hoping that somehow no one gets hurt and that maybe we can all see happy things soon.

They started searching and saw a hideous Snaketia but their main concern was the monsters death. They wanted it more when James told them what he was going to asked Rosecena.

James told them that he was going to have a girlfriend that is a vampire hunter and kill all the other monsters also. That made his brothers and sisters day all except one because she didn't trust Rosecena anyone that could put her family in danger was an enemy of hers. She believed that Rosecena was a major danger because what if they broke up then Rosecena could hunt down James and kill him and that really scared her. Ralph thought that there was no way that Rosecena or James would hurt each other at all.

It was now five o'clock and they was still arguing about rather they thought it was a good idea or not and right away Rosecena snapped and said it doesn't matter what matters is that one way or another the monsters got to go and there's no and if or buts about it. She started to walk away again but she didn't because she thought that she could use their help so she calm herself down and asked them would you please stop arguing so that maybe we can defect the monsters. I just want my family safe and I would like for you guys to be safe also please trust that.

They agreed and started to search again. The monsters were ugly but she just wanted some good news and when she heard the good news that made her day. She knew that she was going to kill them but she didn't know when or how she was going to do it if she had to do it by herself. It would have been hard but with all of them looking that really helped her out and whenever they found the monsters she knew that they would find it weakness also and that would be the end of these monsters. She was praying that it would be soon through because it was taking a lot of energy to handle these monsters and try to keep everything working out as well as can be expected but when she saw that nothing was working out she grew impatient and started worrying because she was just wanting everyone to remain safe.

Who know maybe we can also visit for a while after we kill these monster's, but I don't know you guys always seem to be in such a hurry, thought Rosecena? Then they divided into groups of two, if you find them stab them okay, said Rosecena. Then they began to search on one team was Rosecena and James the rest was up to them. Rosecena and James located the monsters and started to fight them. The others heard the commotion and came to check they were shocked to see the monsters.

They joined in on the fighting and they started to grow frustrated because the monsters weren't dying, and had ran away. She was trying to figure out what to do but she just couldn't. I am so confused she wanted to scream but somehow she keep from doing that she would never say it out loud. Then she asked, them what do they think that they should do now?

They said that they didn't know they never had to deal with creatures like these before. They started to search again because they needed to get rid of these monsters. They started to search but saw that nothing was going as they planned at all. They keep searching because they could tell she was really tired of the monsters.

They didn't like what was going on at all because they knew that all humans needed at least eight hours of sleep at least. They could see that she wasn't getting even that much sleep and that had them all worried. James suggested that she go and sleep but Rosecena was refusing because she was wanting the monsters all dead. She told him that she would sleep when all of these night mares were over. He told her that he knew that she was worried for everyone safety however if she didn't get any sleep she wouldn't be good for anything.

He grew more concerned when she refused to go to sleep. She was just so determined to do what she thought was right rather it was good for her or not. She was going to see the end of the monsters one way or the other. She knew it was possible she just had to believe that and she did with all of her heart.

I'm sorry but I don't think that we can help you with these monsters but if you get hurt then I know that I can help. I'm a doctor and I can get any venom out of you if you will allow me too that is, Ralph said. Thanks, Rosecena said but how can you when my mom is a doctor too. It's because I am a vampire, said Ralph.

Here take this if you get hurt then call me it's got my number programmed and James too. We are still going to try and help but I don't know what we can do? I am going to the library maybe we can find out how to kill it what the monsters name and its weakness. I hope that we can figure out what to do?

Thanks, I hope that we can kill them soon because these monsters are very mean. I am worried that I might get hurt, I know that you are safe through because you a vampire. At least that way, I know that I will be able to fight without you getting hurt. They then started searching again by three o'clock they was all hungry and thirsty so they went and tried to find something to eat the vampires went hunting and then returned.

After they returned, Rosecena and the others started to hunt for the monsters again. Again they found the monsters, this time Rosecena had a planned she had grabbed a trap from her room. She knew that they would be able to use one of those jars to trap them but how to keep her from being poisoned. When she told them that she wanted to try to catch one of these monsters.

James then asked, why should we catch them? Why not just kill them all when we find out how to kill them all? We could catch them and find out their weakness if we capture them, Rosecena said. What do we need that thing for? Why not catch one and then we try to find out what's its weakness is?

If we have one we will be able to learn about them and destroy them once we know its weakness we can come up with an outstanding plan and figure out their weakest form. For example the Kricketia weakness is ice it turns into an egg when its in its weakest then just lock it up.

I hope that we can do the same to these monsters. Why don't you name these creatures since you are the first to see these things, James suggested. We don't know if I am truly the first or not. I don't want to name it and it already has a name.

They then started looking again and tried to put her planned into action when they found them and they succeeded. They caught not one but five and they took them into her room. They put one jar in glue, the other in ink. She put one in darkness, and yet another in flower.

Then the last one she put in water. All at once she notices a reaction from the one in the water. She was glad that they were all in a jar because she didn't know how she was going to catch them if they weren't. Then she heard George yelling for Rosecena to come here its Ralph, he has some information for you.

Rosecena ran to the phone and said, yes you have information, and what is it? These creatures are called Alligatoretia's and they have a lot of venom. They only eat leaves and they love flowers. They only get three feet tall they have snakeheads on their tentacles and they have thorn all over them other than their tentacles and a head of a dolphin.

It has snake fangs in its mouth. That's all I know about them through I'm afraid. I checked every book in here. I'm sorry, I tried my best, I wanted to find out its weakness but there is no information at all about the Alligatoretia, said Ralph. Thanks you so much for finding that out for me.

I am happy to even know that and don't worry we found out its weakness already, said Rosecena. What do you mean? How did you find out? What did I miss?

Rosecena then said calm down. We caught five of the Alligatoretia's and did a little test on them. We now know they hate water. They turned into butterflies when they are in water.

How many butterflies do they turn into? Ralph asked. She then turned the jar over and counted ten. She told him ten and that's only one of those Alligatoretia. That's mean that we will need to catch ten for each of those Alligatoretia.

How are we going to do that Rosecena asked. I don't know, said Ralph maybe you know someone who know about this house, he continued. Rosecena thought about it we need a room where we can flood it and then keep butterflies in it. She then told him I know someone whom just might know.

I'm about to call her, are you coming here, or what? I'm coming to your house, I told you that we will help you with these monsters and I meant it. We are going to kill them and you won't have to worry about your family being in danger any longer after we kill these monsters. That will be great just wish that would come around all ready. It will just be ready because we will have no more worries after it happens. After least then these Alligatoretia's and all the other monsters will be done, you will be safe and so will your family too, say Ralph. Thanks Rosecena said you are really nice. She then called Victoria and asked her about a room they could flood and lock butterflies up in. Why don't you try the flood room, its where king Chris drowned people when he was king it has a lever where you can drain the water.

That's a great idea, thank you would you mind showing me, where that room is right away, please? After they hung up Victoria showed up and showed Rosecena where the room was and where the lever was. She also thought about the secret passage to the room. Rosecena started to try to figure out how to get the monsters in the room.

She was trying her best to figure out a way to trick the monsters into the flood room, but nothing was coming to her. She wanted to make the monster run into the room so that no one can get poisoned. She just wish she knew how because she would be the one who got hurt.

Then she remembers what Ralph told her, that if she got poisoned she could easily get helped thanks to the vampire. She was proud that she was going to get rid of the Alligatoretia's and then she might be able to relax some. They were all trying to come up with a plan to make it go away but no one could come up with it.

Rosecena got aggravated and decided that they had to do whatever they could to get rid of those monsters. She asked would you like to try like we did one time before, or wait till we come up with a plan. They then started to search again and found forty monsters. They started trapping them but what were they going to do if the others escaped then they would know their plans, but how would they catch all of them. Rosecena then got where she didn't care she started to grab them and throw them into the traps. The others saw that and joined her so after a while they counted and somehow fifteen had got away. They had caught twenty-five monsters. She was glad that they caught that many now she wanted those monsters to die, so they took them to the flood room and pulled the lever she was surprised to see the room was flooded then she pulled the level again and the room was filled with butterflies. Now she just wanted to catch the last fifteen, and make them die.

They then decided to go and search for them and destroy them all. They now knew how but they still had one problem to deal with through. You should know that each time you fight these monsters they learn from it. She then told them we still have to deal with the butterflies too, or we can't use the flood room anymore, and I just came up with a plan but we have to trap the butterflies first.

They went to the shed and found a net it was a butterfly net. They were happy to see that because that would make it really easy to catch them, plus then they decided who was going to catch the butterflies. She then asked James if he wanted too.

They all said No, at the same time. Then who going to catch the butterflies then, she asked. Rosecena then made the decision of who was going to catch the butterflies. She grabbed the net and ran into the flood room and closed the door, no butterflies got out of the room.

She was happy to see that but she also wanted to know that those butterflies stay butterflies till they died. She had them all trapped then she called Ralph and them and told them that she needed some jars as soon as possible.

They brought fifty jars. Rosecena then put the twenty-five butterflies in the jars. She then started to try to think of a way to keep the jars from getting broken so she put the jars in the room with the cotton and they there was safe from any monsters. She was proud the monster that was in that room was dead. She knew that it would be safe there and she knew that the monsters wouldn't be able to get away in that room because now almost all the monsters were dead.

She knew that it would be safe there and she knew that the monsters wouldn't be able to get away in that room because now almost all the monsters were dead. She wished that they were all dead through. They all then asked, Rosecena what are they going to do now? They go and start trying to catch the sixteen monsters to kill them she thought. James came up with a plan but to do like they did a little while ago.

They started to search, then found them but instead of being able to grab them and throw them in a jar, they fought back and they stabbed Rosecena's right leg and she started feeling dizzy. She looked down and knew why she felt dizzy right away; she was trying to remain calm so she stood back up and started hunting again. James then noticed that she was hurt he picked her up and took her to Ralph. He showed Ralph where she was stabbed and right away Ralph sucked out all of the venom.

Ralph saved her from dying. She was very glad he was here. Then she came up with a plan. She grabbed a sword and started searching again; when they found the monsters she stabbed them just to make them mad. The monsters then started to chase after Rosecena when she got to the secret room; she stabbed the monsters again and ran into the flood room.

The monsters followed she then yelled hit the switch quickly. All sixteen monsters drowned and turned into butterflies. James then pulled the lever again and the water was gone. He ran to Rosecena, while Rose caught the butterflies. All the monsters were finally dead and everyone survived. She was really happy about the monsters being dead she sat down and they all started talking with her while they were talking to her she accidently fell asleep and they sat there talking with each other while she rested. They didn't want to leave her just in case she got scared and woke up quickly.

She was glad when she woke up and saw James and his family was still there she knew that she was safe and that now she had exactly what she wanted to be there with vampires and a great boyfriend. That really made her day a lot better. She felt really relax sitting down talking with them and then laying down in James lap was even better. George was really watching them hard because he was afraid that the slayer would kill them.

James finally told George not to worry because we are good vampire and she doesn't hurt good vampires. That made George relaxes a whole lot more than he expected. Now you know and you guys can go home or whatever if you want to. They all started to relax but they didn't know how long that would be.

They talked for hours and when James and his family started to decide to leave Rosecena asked him to come and see her again whenever he wanted to because she enjoyed his company a lot. She started to invite him to come with her to Russia whenever she was going but she decided not to because she would have enough on her plate to deal with all ready. She decided not to tell James about her trip to Russia. Ralph then asked what do you plan to do after you tell your family that it is safe for them to come home. I don't know maybe have some fun and then I'm planning to get the rest I need and then catch up on my school work. Maybe after that go destroy more evil creatures.

Oh that's sounds wonderful said Ralph. I am hoping to return home catch up on my rest and protect my family as much as possible. That's sounds great too but thanks to you guys I don't have to worry about my family being in danger anymore and I am really thankful for that. She was really happy because she was getting a lot of good things going her way now and she knew that catching up on her school work was going to be easy.

They went to twilight to go and relax and get some relaxation she was going to enjoy some time without monsters. They stayed till four or five and then they had to go and she didn't like that at all because she wanted them to stay and hang out for a very long time. She really understood that they couldn't stay and hang out with her longer. They left and she decided that she needed to call her family and tell them the good news they were really happy when the phone rang and she told her parents that it was safe for them to come home and hang out with her.

Her parents came home and asked Rosecena would you like to go and have some fun now. Right away she told them yes I need to get out and relax some more. They went to twilight and ate some good food and then they went to the circus and went and have more fun. They had an amazing time that night that when Rosecena got home she fell right asleep and rested all through the night her family was very pleased that she got to enjoy time with them and she was resting.

The following night she went with her family to watch Titanic and also went to a concert. She had another great night and she had almost forgot that she had to go to Russia but she had it wrote down on her schedule. She went to her room and started writing books down that she was going to bring with her while in Russia. She had five books on her mind that she was going to bring and she was glad of that because it was going to be hard enough to bring all of the things that she was going to have to deal with and all the things for taking out all of the monsters also.

While she was in Russia she was determined that she was going to get it all handle as fast as possible. She was going to have all her favorite clothes, her books and her favorite weapons also. She was nervous because she didn't want to be the one that had to deal with all these creatures because she was only one person and there were so many creatures. She was tired of all the monsters and every other creature also. She didn't know how she was going to defeat all the creatures but she didn't know how.

Rosecena was trying to do her best to make everything perfect again some how. James could see something was bothering his girlfriend so he asked what was up. Rosecena didn't want to tell him but she just gave up and told him that she was tired and she didn't want to worry him. She then asked James if he would come and lay down with her in till her family got home and then he could leave or just stay and hang out either way.

James agreed and stayed with her she was so glad that he was with her.

James was refusing to leave Rosecena because he was worried about her and he knew something was differently wrong. She was glad that the monsters was all dead or locked up and she was glad that she was going to get to relax and maybe make the world safe for everyone one step at a time.

The very thought of that really made her proud of herself and even other people who helped her with all of the monsters and every other creatures in the universe. They went to her bed room and she started to relax and she was about to fall asleep when she heard the doorbell ring. It was her family she was kind of worried when they used the doorbell and she asked them why they didn't just come in to the house. When they said that they did it just to make her worried she got kind of annoyed because she had a lot on her mind and she was really tired already.

Rosecena then went back to her bedroom and she fell asleep. They was really happy to see that she was finally relaxing and getting to do what she needed to do. After she slept that night she went to where her family was and she started to tell her family that she was about to go and pack to get ready to go to Russia. She really didn't want to go but she knew that she had to go. She really wanted to stay at the palace and relax for a while.

She knew that she needed to go and handle the monsters and she knew that something was going to happen when she went to Russia. She was very glad that she was about to get the break that she needed and she was praying that this was the end of all of her problems. She knew that it wasn't but still she could still hope for the best. She decided that it was time to go and handle the rest of the problems.

She decided that while she had the chance she would go and looked up the monsters while she had a library. She found all of the monsters except one of them. It was werewolves which kind of upset her because she had limited knowledge about them. She now knew a little bit of information about the giants but she didn't know how to kill them.

She started to read the other books but most of the vampire's book told her stuff she already knew. She then looked at the wizard books and found a way to deal with him. She was going through all of the books. All of the books told her a little information she didn't know except the vampire's book.

After the library, she went to heading home but met up with a few friends and hung out with them. She was glad to be able to do that because it was way overdue. She was enjoying herself when she remembers that she needed to go home and start to pack she had to also get her parents to turn in the books because she wasn't going to be in town soon.

She headed home and started to think about all the stuff she needed to pack. She packed and then she went down stairs with her parents and sisters. She asked them if there was anything else she forgot, and they said "No," I hope that you are safe while you are gone. They all hugged and then Rosecena started on her way to the airport.

THE END OR IS IT, WHAT IS REALLY THE END OF ANYTHING?

CPSIA information can be obtained
at www.ICGtesting.com
Printed in the USA
JSHW020749260722
28503JS00002B/10